## "How do you feel— about marriage?"

Her employer's unexpected question stunned Jill, totally disconcerting her. "What do you mean?" she said warily.

"I was simply wondering if marriage had any part in your scheme of things—or do you plan to be solely a career girl?

"No marriage for me," Jill said firmly. "Not for a long time yet; I like being free too much."

"But you thought *I* should marry again...."

"I only meant it would be good for your son if you *did* marry again!"

"But you're not volunteering for the job?"

Jill raised stunned blue eyes in answer. "Don't worry," Luke drawled mockingly, "I wasn't proposing. As you've already pointed out, I'm very much older than you and I'm no cradle snatcher."

**KATE WALKER** chose the Brontë sisters, the development of their writing from childhood to maturity, as the topic for her master's thesis. It is little wonder, then, that she should go on to write romance fiction. She lives in the United Kingdom with her husband and son, and when she isn't writing, she tries to keep up with her hobbies of embroidery, knitting, antiques and, of course, reading.

## Books by Kate Walker

HARLEQUIN ROMANCE
2783—GAME OF HAZARD
2826—ROUGH DIAMOND

# KATE WALKER

## broken silence

**_Harlequin Books_**

TORONTO • NEW YORK • LONDON
AMSTERDAM • PARIS • SYDNEY • HAMBURG
STOCKHOLM • ATHENS • TOKYO • MILAN

for
PAT
who was there at the beginning

Harlequin Presents first edition February 1988
ISBN 0-373-11053-7

Original hardcover edition published in 1987
by Mills & Boon Limited

# CHAPTER ONE

'YOU *are* Miss Carpenter?'

Was it only her mood, Jill wondered, or did those words really have a sharply hostile tone that seemed to catch on her already rather frayed nerves? She was ill-prepared for any such reaction, feeling hot and sticky and tired after a decidedly unsettling journey, and when she had expected to be met by the elderly, dignified Mrs Logan it had come as something of a shock to be accosted by an unknown and apparently unfriendly man.

'You're very late,' he said accusingly, dark blue eyes narrowing critically as he subjected her to a coolly appraising survey of her appearance. The frankly disapproving glance that took in her pink jeans and brightly checked shirt was positively the last straw.

'I know I'm late!' Jill snapped tartly, and knew from the perceptible tightening of his firm straight lips that her sharp response had been a mistake. 'I couldn't help it,' she amended hastily.

One eyebrow, fair like his hair, lifted slightly, questioning either her words or her tone—or both—then a slight nod, little more than an inclination of his head, dismissed the matter as he held out his hand.

'I'm Luke,' he said, and there seemed to be the slightest hesitation before he gave his name. Not even the faintest flicker of a polite smile accompanied his words and the deep blue eyes remained as coolly indifferent as before.

'The car's over there.'

Luke nodded in the direction of the sleek silver-grey Mercedes that had been the first thing Jill had seen as she had alighted from the bus at the end of her jolting,

7

uncomfortable journey, though, expecting Anne
Logan's Rover, she hadn't connected it with Stoneroyd
House. There had been no one in the car, the courtyard
of the Wheatsheaf Inn apparently being deserted, and
Jill had been trying to resign herself to the prospect of
the three-mile walk from Sorley village to Stoneroyd
when Luke had come up behind her.

Her stomach twisting in an echo of her own startled
reaction to that moment, she followed Luke as he walked
silently towards the car. Obviously a man of few words,
our Luke, she thought wryly, which did nothing to ease
the tension and unease that had been tying her stomach
in knots with the feeling that today had been jinxed from
the start. A wave of embarrassment washed over her at
the thought of the way she had jumped like a startled cat
when Luke's long shadow had fallen across the gravel,
spinning round to stare foolishly, so thoroughly disconcerted that she had been unable to frame an answer to his
curt demand to know if she was the Miss Carpenter he
was to meet, so that he had had to repeat the question, a
rising note of anger in his voice.

He moved round to the other side of the car, sliding in
beside her and leaning forward to insert the key into the
ignition. His sudden closeness and an unexpected and
overwhelming awareness of the controlled strength of
the hard body next to hers made her heart jolt
uncomfortably. She had no idea of Luke's exact position
at Stoneroyd, but some intuitive sense told her that, no
matter who he was, he would make a bad enemy if
crossed, a thought which had her blundering hastily into
belated apology.

'I'm sorry I was so late. I missed the bus I was meant
to catch and there was no way to let anyone know.'

Which was not exactly *her* fault, a small, rebellious
voice added inside her head. Stoneroyd's phone number
was ex-directory and the only contact she had had with
the house and its occupants had come by post or through

Mrs Logan, who had always telephoned Jill herself. Apart from Danny, Anne Logan was the only person she knew at Stoneroyd, which was why she had been completely thrown by this man's unexpected appearance.

Just who *was* he? He had told her nothing beyond that one fact that his name was Luke, and even that had been given with reluctance. She felt as if she was operating completely in the dark, with not even the faintest pinprick of light to guide her.

'My father's car broke down,' Jill continued her explanation, forcing herself to ignore the discouraging silence of the man at her side. She owed him this at least.

Determinedly she squashed down a pang of regret for her half-formed hope that Danny might have come to meet her with his grandmother. She would have felt so much better then. Danny had been her main reason for taking this job in the face of her parents' disapproval and lack of understanding. There had been other, more personal reasons for her decision, but they had faded into insignificance from the moment she had met the bright-eyed, dark-haired six-year-old bundle of mischief who had accompanied Anne Logan to the interview in Burnbridge two weeks before. The little boy had stolen her heart from the first and everything she had learned about him since had made her more determined to take the position as his nanny, even if the post was only temporary, lasting no more than three months.

'By the time we got it going again, the bus that got me here at three had left. I had to get the one after that.'

Luke turned his head to look at her, his deep blue eyes expressionless.

'I shouldn't worry about it. It's a pleasant day and I filled the time quite easily.'

The words came politely enough, bland, social phrases meant to put her at her ease, but something

about his voice, a stiffness in his tone, and the
deliberateness with which he turned his attention firmly
back to his driving after he had spoken, sent a prickling
irritation running down Jill's spine. There was something else too, a hint of something carefully concealed in
that swift glance that made her acutely conscious of her
rather dishevelled appearance.

With a faint sigh she pushed one hand through her
short blonde hair, grimacing in distaste at the feel of the
damp strands of her fringe clinging to her fingers.

Her fine fair hair had an unfortunate tendency to
become limp very quickly in warm weather and even
though she had washed it only that morning she was
painfully aware of the way it was already clinging to the
delicate bones of her skull, lank and straight as a ruler,
with no redeeming hint of a wave.

It was impossible not to contrast Luke's appearance
with her own. In spite of the heat he looked cool and
relaxed, his white shirt crisp and immaculate unlike her
rather crumpled cotton blouse and the thick fair hair
which he wore brushed back from his face was anything
but limp. Several shades lighter than Jill's, silver where
hers was gold, its gleaming crispness revealed a strong
tendency to wave, to fall just where it wanted in spite of
careful and probably expensive styling.

Luke's movement as he changed gear smoothly drew
her eyes to his left hand, seeing for the first time the
thick gold band on the third finger. So Mr Luke was
married. She wondered briefly what Mrs Luke would be
like, but found it impossible to guess.

She didn't ask, however. It was already quite clear
that this man was not the type to tolerate personal
questions on such short acquaintance—if ever, she
added with a sidelong glance at his uncommunicative
profile. Still, perhaps she'd better try to make conversation. She didn't intend to sit in silence for the entire
journey—and there was plenty she wanted to know

about the house that was to be her home for the next three months—and even more about the people who lived in it.

'Will Mr Garrett be at home today?' she asked, deliberately choosing the subject of the one occupant of Stoneroyd about whom the least was known—Danny's father and her employer.

There was no response from the silent figure beside her, but she was not going to give in that easily.

'I thought he'd want to see me. After all, it's his son I'll be looking after, and he probably knows very little about me—not much more than I know about him.' Curiosity overcame her. 'What *does* he do?'

For a moment she thought Luke was not going to answer her and was frankly startled when at last he spoke.

'Music recording and publishing,' he said briefly.

It was Jill's turn to be silent as she digested this piece of information. It wasn't quite what she had expected, though, if challenged, she probably wouldn't have been able to say just what she *had* expected. She had been away at college when the Garretts had moved into Stoneroyd House, but had heard about the new arrivals on her return home for the Christmas holidays, mainly from Mrs Dawson who ran the local post office and knew everything about everybody, often before they knew themselves.

From her Jill had learned that Garrett was a widower, his wife having died when his son Danny was only six months old, and that the little boy was cared for by his maternal grandmother, Anne Logan, because his father spent most of his time in London, returning only for infrequent and irregular weekends.

Beyond that, even Mary Dawson knew very little. Mrs Logan and little Daniel had been seen out shopping in Burnbridge and were quite well known to most of the local tradesmen, but of Mr Garrett himself there had been no sign. In Mary Dawson's words, 'he kept himself to himself' and was considered a recluse and something of a mystery. There were rumours of visitors at Stoneroyd too, 'arty types' with big cars who came up for weekends and occasionally ventured into town, instantly recognisable by their expensively fashionable clothes and free and easy ways with money.

The car moved on up a steep, winding hill. They were well away from Sorley now, the village just a cluster of tiny houses halfway down the valley. Jill looked about her with interest. Stoneroyd House could not be far away. It was set almost on the edge of the moors and they were out in the country already, green fields and stone walls all that she could see. It was only when the road dipped down again and Sorley was hidden from sight that she realised how carefully Luke had avoided telling her anything at all beyond that one fact that her employer worked in the music business.

A wry smile touched her lips at the thought of how little she had actually discovered about Garrett himself. Whoever Luke was, he was certainly discreet—excessively so in Jill's opinion. He obviously had no intention of discussing his employer with anyone, certainly not some newly-arrived, temporary help.

She was distracted from her thoughts as the car swung suddenly left, past a pair of high wrought iron gates, and up a slight slope, and at last the house was in sight.

# CHAPTER TWO

'OH, but it's lovely!' Jill exclaimed, looking round her in delight. The exterior of Stoneroyd House had been imposing but bleak. A typical example of northern architecture, built for strength rather than show, its grey stone blended easily with the dark moors behind it. Stone steps led up to a great wooden door set exactly between the two front bay windows and a glass-covered conservatory built on to one side was the only relief from its sombre solidity.

But inside the house was bright and welcoming and the bedroom to which Luke had led her, although small in comparison to some of the downstairs rooms, seemed airy and spacious when contrasted with her own cramped bedroom at home. Decorated in gold and white, it positively glowed in the light of the sun that poured in through the window.

'There's a sitting-room and kitchen through here.' Luke had opened a door at the far end of the room, standing aside so that Jill could see through it.

She had a swift impression of a large, comfortable room with a big bay window overlooking the garden at the back of the house. It was furnished in bright primary colours, clearly intended to act as Danny's nursery as well as the sitting-room Luke had called it. A settee and armchairs were gathered round an open fireplace, there was a dining table and chairs, already showing signs of being well used as a six-year-old's play table too, and in one corner was a tiny kitchenette with fridge, cooker, sink and cupboards. Against the wall opposite the windows stood a huge cupboard filled to overflowing with toys, books and games.

'Daniel uses this room as his playroom,' Luke was saying. 'His room's just across the landing. There's a bathroom too, and Anne's—Mrs Logan's—bedroom and sitting-room.'

'It looks quite perfect.' Jill made herself say it, but her heart wasn't in the words. There was nothing wrong with the room—it *was* perfect, providing everything a small boy needed—materially at least.

'Where is Danny?' Jill asked now. She had been frankly surprised by the silence of the house, the absence of any sign of life, having hoped—expected—that as soon as the car had come to a halt the big main door would open and the little boy would come rushing out to greet her.

'He's gone out for the day. As a matter of fact he won't be back until tomorrow. Anne took him to spend the night with some friends of hers. She thought you might like a little time to settle in on your own, get to know the place without Danny to cope with too. They should be back about noon tomorrow.' Luke glanced at his watch. 'I expect you'd like to unpack and freshen up. We don't eat before eight, usually, when Danny's in bed, so shall I see about some tea or something? You could have it in the garden in, say, half an hour—unless you'd prefer it up here?'

'In the garden would be lovely.' Jill's voice sounded satisfactorily even in spite of the struggle she was having to bite back the flippant comment that this was the longest speech she had ever heard him make that was burning on her tongue. She had already classified Luke as the strong, silent type.

'Well, come down when you're ready. The door on the left at the bottom of the stairs will take you into the garden. I'll ask Mrs Jenkins to have some tea ready about five.'

And really, for Luke, that was quite amazingly friendly, Jill told herself with dry flippancy as she heard his footsteps descend the stairs, the knot of tension that still held her muscles taut easing as the sound died away. She wasn't at all sure just why this particular man should have this unnerving effect on her, but there was something about him that just seemed to rub her up the wrong way. She had only spent half an hour in his company, but already she felt that, unless things changed dramatically, she would never be completely comfortable in his presence.

Still, perhaps Mrs Luke would be more friendly, she thought as she turned her attention to the suitcase Luke had left on the bed. Luke himself was obviously quite a lot older than herself—she guessed his age at something over thirty—but his wife could be some years younger and stuck out here, miles from anywhere, might be glad of some company.

The door at the bottom of the stairs led into a large, sunny room from which sliding glass doors opened on to a terrace on which stood a wooden table and chairs, the table already laid with tea things. Jill wandered out on to the terrace, then stared in amazement at the garden that lay spread out before her. She had known that Garrett was wealthy, but she had never expected anything quite as magnificent as this!

Just below the terrace was a huge, immaculate lawn bordered by carefully tended flowerbeds. A low stone wall with a gate set into it separated this from a neatly cultivated area stocked with rows of vegetables and fruit bushes, and beyond that was a shady, tree-filled area where Jill could just see the sparkle of a stream flowing at the foot of the hill that rose up behind the house. To her left, carefully fenced off, was a fair-sized swimming pool looking cool and welcoming in the heat of the late afternoon.

She stood for a moment revelling in the sheer space and colour of it all, then amongst the trees she caught the flash of a white shirt and heard a dog's deep bark and a

few moments later Luke was striding towards her, the
dog at his heels—no, there were two of them now, both
wolfhounds and almost indistinguishable from each
other except that one was perhaps slightly smaller than
the other—but not much, she thought wryly, unable to
suppress the wish that if Luke had to have dogs as pets he
could at least have chosen something less enormous.

'You found your way all right, then?' Luke mounted
the short flight of steps to the terrace, taking them two at
a time, and came to stand beside the table just as she sat
down at it.

'No trouble.'

Jill wished he would sit down. His height was
decidedly unnerving as he towered over her, his back to
the sun so that she had to squint unflatteringly against
its glare and even then could not make out his features
clearly.

'Would you like some tea?' She couldn't help the way
the words sounded, coming out with stiff formality as if
she was forcing herself to be polite, her uncertainty as to
just how to take this man showing in her voice.

Luke shook his head. 'Not for me, thanks, but you go
ahead.'

Jill did just that, savouring the welcome drink and
privately getting her thoughts back into proportion as
she did so.

'The swimming pool is at your disposal any time you
want to use it,' Luke was saying. 'Danny loves it. He'd
stay in all day if he could.'

'I'd enjoy that too,' Jill said, her mind not on her
words but on the realisation that a tiny hint of warmth
had crept into the emotionless voice when Luke spoke of
Danny, making her smile secretly to herself. So even
cool Luke had succumbed to the little boy's charms! She
was glad of that, it made him seem a little more human at
least, and perhaps, just perhaps she could turn the
affection he felt for Danny to her advantage. If she could

win one person at Stoneroyd round to her way of thinking, she might be able to make some changes. 'It must be a real luxury to have your own pool, especially in weather like this. In fact the whole house is quite beautiful. Mr Garrett must miss it when he's in London.'

'He does.'

Luke didn't look at her as he spoke, his deep blue gaze fixed firmly on the tops of the trees at the bottom of the garden—and perhaps it was just as well that he didn't because he missed the slightly sceptical expression that crossed Jill's face at his words. Privately she very much doubted that Garrett missed anything at all of his home life when he was away, at least not if his obsession with his work was as all-pervading as it was reputed to be. He must be in the capital today too, she had seen no sign of his presence in the house.

In an effort to hide her betraying face she bent her head to look at the two dogs, both seeming slightly less imposing now that they lay in the shade of the table, heads on paws. Cautiously she held out a tentative hand towards the smaller of the two, only to be brought upright sharply by the sudden sound of Luke's voice.

'Tara and Minstrel aren't pets, Miss Carpenter. They're guard dogs officially—very efficient ones too—and I'd be obliged if you'd treat them as such.'

'Isn't that rather dangerous?' The words came jerkily, as much from dislike of the cold, commanding way Luke spoke as from annoyance at the way he had startled her. 'I mean, what about Danny? Is he safe with such animals around?'

'Perfectly.' Luke's tone was clipped and curt. 'They can be trusted absolutely where he's concerned, they'd not hurt anyone they know.'

Once more Jill caught that hard, warning note in his voice and wondered at it. He need have no worries about her treatment of the dogs, she already had a healthy

respect for their size and strength that would prevent
her from ever being too inclined to treat them as pets,
but it was the unspoken words implied behind what he
had said that worried her. The wolfhounds might be
trustworthy with people they knew, but what about
unwary strangers or intruders? She felt a cold shiver run
down her spine at the thought that Garrett's need for
absolute privacy had turned Stoneroyd into an isolated
fortress, guarded by the two great dogs. Just what had
made her employer so obsessed with his own security?

Luke moved suddenly, lowering himself into the seat
beside her and stretching his long muscular legs out in
front of him, and although only minutes before she had
wanted him to do just that now, perversely, she wished
with an irrational intensity that he had stayed where he
was. One long-fingered hand lay on the arm of his chair,
disturbingly close to her own, and a sudden feeling of
breathlessness, the jolting of her heart into a new jerky
pattern in an instinctive reaction to his nearness
reminded her of the moment in the car when she had
become so intensely sensitive to the potent force of his
masculine strength so that she couldn't feel comfortable
sitting next to him, her throat closing over the words she
had been about to speak to break the stiff little silence
that had descended between them. Every nerve seemed
to quiver with newly heightened awareness so that she
started nervously when Luke spoke unexpectedly.

'I understand you've just left college,' he said, and Jill
found herself failing in her newly formed resolve not to
overreact as she mentally considered his tone, testing it
to see if that inexplicable hostility was still there.
Finding nothing but a cool politeness, she relaxed a
little.

'That's right. I was at library school in Aberystwyth.'

'Looking after Danny won't be exactly what you'd
planned on doing, then?'

It was a perfectly reasonable question; he wasn't to

know that this was a particularly touchy subject. The wonderful job her parents had anticipated so confidently hadn't materialised after months of applications and interviews. It wasn't that Jill had expected it to be handed to her on a plate, she was well aware of the fact that in Burnbridge she was a rarity, one of the few amongst the younger generation who had gone to college at all, but in Aberystwyth she had been just one of hundreds, all aiming for the same goal, and now all competing for the few jobs that were available.

'Not exactly,' she said carefully. 'But library jobs are a bit thin on the ground at the moment and I need to be earning some money.'

And that was one of the points over which she and her parents had disagreed. They had been perfectly content to let her live with them, not in the least concerned that she couldn't contribute adequately to the cost of her keep, and happy to have her there until a 'proper job' turned up. But Jill had been restless. Her days at college had given her an independence that jarred with the life of a dependent daughter living at home. She was used to coping for herself, living her own life, and even the few restrictions that were the result of living in her parents' house had soon begun to fret at her, so that when she had heard that Mrs Logan needed someone to care for Danny while she was away it had seemed the perfect answer.

'I can't live off Mum and Dad, money's tight enough as it is. Dad lost a lot of business when he was laid up with a bad back earlier this year, so I can't expect them to support me.'

'Very independent of you,' Luke remarked lazily, but his eyes belied the drawl of his voice. Under the hooded lids they were fixed on her face and his intent scrutiny disturbed her.

'Well, I——' she began, but again he silenced her with a gesture.

'Don't be so indignant. I meant it as a compliment.'

'Oh!' Jill's irritation subsided as quickly as it had arisen, leaving her shaken and ill at ease. Something that was almost a smile hovered around Luke's lips, and that only made matters worse, revealing only too clearly that he was well aware of how much his words had disconcerted her—and she had a strong suspicion that he had planned that they should do just that. Hastily she sought for something that would move the conversation on to a less personal topic.

'Tell me about Danny,' she said impulsively. 'What's he really like?'

A picture formed in her mind as she spoke, Danny as she had first seen him, too neat, too controlled, too formally polite for a six-year-old. He had relaxed later, after some hard work on her part, and had chattered away quite cheerfully, but underneath that flow of conversation Jill had sensed a restraint, an inner loneliness that had reinforced her belief that, although Mrs Logan had done her best to fill the emptiness left by the death of his mother, Danny had suffered from having an almost non-existent father too.

'Danny.' Luke linked his hands together in an arch, considering her question. 'He's a typical six-year-old, on the go from morning till night. I hope you've got plenty of energy because, believe me, you're going to need it!'

'I understand he's devoted to his father,' Jill said tentatively, trying to bring the conversation round to Garrett as tactfully as possible. She had no desire to spark off the volcano she suspected was only slumbering under Luke's newly affable surface.

'Yes.' The single syllable was deliberately discouraging, but she determined to ignore that.

'Does Mr Garrett get home often?'

The hands that had been lightly clasped tightened perceptibly.

'Not often enough,' Luke said shortly. 'He's not here as much as Danny needs him to be.'

She had been right. There *was* some affection for Danny there—and perhaps some hostility towards his employer too. Certainly that touch of bitterness in his voice made such an interpretation possible. She might win Luke round as an ally yet.

'Why doesn't he come more frequently?' she asked without stopping to think if the question was wise or not. 'Surely he knows Danny needs him so much—more so because he doesn't have a mother.'

'I think you'll find he's well aware of that.' The quiet voice held an ominous thread of warning, a warning Jill was too concerned to heed.

'Then why doesn't he do something about it?'

'He has his business interests to consider.' Luke's voice was even quieter now, dangerously so. 'They provide for Danny.'

'*Materially.*' She made no attempt to hide her scorn and indignation. 'I'll grant you that Garrett manages that side of things very well,' she rushed on, thinking of the overflowing toy cupboard upstairs, the swimming pool, a new bicycle she could see in the garden. 'Danny has everything money can buy—everything he could want—but in *things* only. Children need much more than that. They need time and love and and——'

Luke's frozen stillness made her falter in mid-flow. He hadn't said a word, hadn't even looked at her, but she could feel his hostility like cold rain on the air, making her shiver involuntarily.

'Go on,' he said when she hesitated. 'You obviously want to get something off your chest. What *do* children need?' he prompted coldly when, unable to read either his tone or his expression, she found herself incapable of continuing.

Oh well, she decided with a mental shrug, she might as well be hanged for a sheep as a lamb.

'They need to know their parents love them—that they'll be there when they need them. When I was young money was very tight. Dad was just setting up his own decorating business and there wasn't much cash to spare for toys or new clothes—but my parents were always around, for a cuddle, for advice if we needed it, or just for a chat—they were always *there*!'

'You obviously had a very happy childhood.' Luke had his voice rigidly under control, each word icy hard, falling into the silence like splinters of glass. 'Not everyone's that lucky.'

Without warning he raised his head and looked straight into Jill's face, his eyes as bleak and unfriendly as a winter sea, sending a frisson of fear feathering over her nerves at the realisation that under that controlled façade burned a cold fury that she almost felt could shrivel her into dust where she sat.

'I'll give you this warning just once,' he went on harshly. 'Leave Garrett alone. He's arranged things as he wants them, he won't take kindly to anyone interfering. So if you've any ideas of trying to change things here, for Danny's sake or anyone else's, I should forget them now. Is that understood?'

Jill could only nod numbly as Luke got to his feet. She had meant to try so hard, take things so very carefully, and yet in spite of all her good resolutions she had still managed to set a light to his explosive temper.

'Now if you'll excuse me I have work to do.' The stiff politeness of Luke's tone was belied by the white marks of anger around his nose and mouth, his eyes darkened to a deep midnight-blue by rigidly controlled emotion. 'When you've finished your tea perhaps you could take the tray through into the kitchen and introduce yourself to Jenky—Mrs Jenkins. I expect she'll be glad to see you. It's a bit quiet up here for her at times.'

And when do I get to meet your wife? Jill wondered, but Luke was already moving away, leaving her in no doubt that now was not the time to ask and giving her no option but to go along with the programme he had suggested.

*Suggested!* She repeated the word to herself satirically. From anyone else it would have been a suggestion, but Luke managed to give even the most casual request the force of a command as if he expected her to jump to immediate attention at his slightest word, and the scarcely disguised relief with which he had left her was decidedly insulting. Well, you're not the only one, Mr Luke whoever you are, she told the absent Luke silently as she loaded the tea things on to the tray. To tell the truth, I don't care for *your* company much either!

# CHAPTER THREE

WELL, like Luke's company or not, you're in for another dose of it tonight, Jill told herself two hours later as she luxuriated in the bath.

The time she had spent with Mrs Jenkins—or Jenky as the housekeeper insisted she called her, using Danny's pet name that had been adopted by the whole family—had been thoroughly enjoyable, a relaxed interlude in the middle of the uneasy tension of the rest of the day. They had shared a fresh pot of tea and a long, companionable chat, Jill passing on all the news and the latest gossip from Burnbridge, in the hope of gradually being able to bring the conversation around to the subject of Luke, his wife—and the mysterious Mr Garrett.

But the pot of tea had been drained before Jenky even slowed her flow of questions and, well before she was ready, Jill had been bustled out of the kitchen with instructions to get ready for dinner.

'You'll need time to freshen up and get changed. Mrs Logan likes the evening meal to be a fairly formal occasion, a chance for the family to get together when Danny's in bed. I usually serve dinner just after eight— it won't be anything fancy tonight, not with Mrs L out visiting—and everyone meets in the garden room—the one at the bottom of your staircase—about half an hour before that, for a drink. So you see you'll have to get your skates on if you're going to be ready in time.'

She hadn't exactly come prepared for any sort of dressing for dinner, Jill reflected as she rubbed herself dry, mentally reviewing the collection of clothes she had brought with her as she did so. She had expected that, once Mrs Logan had left on her trip to Canada where she would be visiting her son, she and Danny would eat all their meals together and that her evenings would be spent on her own—indeed, she had brought a large supply of books with her in order to fill those quiet hours. Now it seemed she was to socialise with the other members of the household, notably the unapproachable Luke.

Luke. Jill's hand stilled on the Indian print skirt she had selected as being the smartest item in her limited wardrobe, a frown creasing her forehead as she thought back over the uncomfortable scene on the terrace. Did Luke's hostile attitude have any connection with that last, cryptic comment Mrs Logan had made at the end of her interview?

It was after she had been offered the job, when they had discussed wages, time off, and other practical matters, that Danny's grandmother had given Jill a thoughtful, considering look and asked abruptly, 'What do you know of Daniel's father—Mr Garrett?'

'Not a lot,' Jill had answered honestly, rather taken aback by the question. 'He works in London, doesn't he?'

Anne Logan nodded slowly. 'I doubt if you'll see very much of him. He may be home some weekends, but he's very busy at the moment. He likes to see as much of Daniel as he can when he is at home.'

'Of course,' Jill had agreed, her face revealing nothing of her private thoughts.

'Danny was too young to know anything when his mother died—he doesn't remember her, of course.' Mrs Logan's face saddened as she spoke of her dead daughter. 'But he's devoted to his father.' She glanced at Jill again, a touch of anxiety clouding her eyes. 'I'm taking something of a risk employing you. Daniel's father wanted someone older, more mature, but I'm satisfied that you'll be able to handle the job. After what you've told me about your sister's twin girls, one small boy shouldn't be too much of a problem. And you and Danny get on so well together—I'm sure he'll come round,' she went on more decisively. 'In a way, perhaps your youth could be an advantage.'

Jill shook her head slowly. She had thought over that last, mysterious remark often since that day, more than a little puzzled by what it might mean. She couldn't see what her age had to do with anything, though she had to acknowledge that if Garrett had planned on employing a mature, middle-aged woman to care for his son then she, with her twenty-first birthday still a few weeks away, would not be at all what he wanted. And if Luke shared his employer's opinion on that matter then——

She broke off her train of thought abruptly, her hands stilling on the tiny pearl buttons of the white blouse as a new thought surfaced with a sudden, shocking clarity so that it seemed impossible she hadn't considered it before. After Mrs Logan's comments on her age, she had visualised Danny's father as a man in his mid-forties, a man who had become a father late in life and who had somewhat old-fashioned ideas about the way his child should be brought up—but if *Luke* was Garrett——!

The idea, once considered, took root in her mind, sending reverberations out from that one central point like the ripples flowing from a stone thrown into a pond. She recalled that hesitation before he gave his name, the careful avoidance of any surname to go with that abrupt 'Luke', his anger when she had criticised Garrett—oh, lord! The things she'd said!

No! Jill caught herself up sharply. She stuck by everything she said. No matter who Luke was or wasn't, she had meant every single word of it, and if he *was* Garrett he had only himself to blame if he'd heard things he didn't like. Mrs Logan hadn't employed that mature, older woman her son-in-law had wanted, she told herself determinedly, she'd employed her and, con-

vinced as she was that a younger, more relaxed approach
to life was what Danny needed, she was quite prepared
to stick to her guns even if her employer and the
objectionable Luke did turn out to be one and the same
person!

The garden room was empty when Jill entered it, the
patio doors still open to allow a faint breeze into the
room, bringing a welcome coolness after the heavy heat
of the day. Idly Jill wandered round, studying the
room's contents to see if they would give her some
insight into the character of the man who owned the
house, some clue as to whether her suspicions about
Luke were correct.

An elaborate stereo and tape deck stood on a table at
one side of the room, the rack underneath stacked with
records and cassettes, most of the latter with no labels on
to indicate their contents other than a hastily scribbled
date. Jill frowned, puzzled, but then she recalled Luke's
curt 'Music recording and publishing'—what sort of
music? Impelled by curiosity, she slipped a cassette into
the machine and switched it on, wandering away again
to lean against the open doors, looking out on to the
garden as the music filled the room, a man's voice,
husky, powerful and yet capable of a haunting gentleness that made her sense that the singer had really felt
the emotions described in the song. It was strangely
familiar too, tugging at her memory, reminding her——
*Where* had she heard it before?

Her reverie was broken into abruptly when the
cassette was switched off without warning and in the
sudden silence Jill swung round, coming face to face
with Luke, who had come into the room unnoticed. He
had changed into navy trousers and a deep blue shirt, the
colour of his clothes making his hair seem almost silver
by contrast and heightening the blue of his eyes. Jill
risked one glance into their smoulderingly angry depths
and immediately wished she hadn't. Instinctively she

took a step backwards as if trying to move out of range of
his fury. What had she done now?

'I'd prefer if it you left things alone in here,' Luke
declared harshly. 'Particularly that.' A violent gesture
indicated the stereo.

If he'd stopped there, stunned shock and a distinctly
fearful twisting sensation in her stomach might have
kept her from retaliating; she might even have apolo-
gised. But Luke continued, his voice clipped and hard as
his anger warred against the control he was imposing,
'In fact, I'd appreciate it if you didn't meddle with
anything.'

And that came too close to his earlier accusation of
prying, setting a light to the touch-paper of Jill's own
temper, making it flare to match his so that for the
moment she forgot her doubts and suspicions.

'I'll take my instructions from my employer—Mr
Garrett—not you!'

Her outburst brought Luke up sharp, just for a
moment, his dark eyes narrowing swiftly as he shot her
one brief, assessing glance. When he spoke his voice was
freezing cold, his words dousing her anger as swiftly as it
had burst into flames.

'I think you'll find that Garrett and I are in complete
agreement over this and you would be wise to take my
instructions as his. He's not a man who likes his privacy
invaded.'

That's been made perfectly clear! Jill was tempted to
flash back, but she swallowed the retort down hastily and
concentrated instead on trying to think straight,
clear her mind of the anger that clouded it, because that
momentary hesitation, so like the one before he had
given her his name, had brought the suspicion that he
might actually *be* Garrett rushing back in full force.
There was one question that might clear up the problem
once and for all—if she could find the nerve to ask it.

Taking a deep breath, she brought the words out in a rush.

'Will your wife be joining us tonight?'

That brought those dark eyes swinging round to her, blazing with such a savage hostility that her blood seemed to freeze in fear, the silence in the room growing deeper and more threatening with every second that passed until, after one brief glance down at his left hand, Luke spoke at last.

'No, my wife will not be joining us,' he said stiffly. 'Not tonight or any other night——' He seemed about to go on, then evidently changed his mind and continued with a bewildering change of tone, 'Would you like sherry or would you prefer something else?'

'Sherry, please.' It was an effort to get the words out, she was so thoroughly disconcerted by the way he could switch from one mood to another, leaving her still caught up in the feelings of the first one.

Snatching the moment while Luke's back was turned, she studied him more closely, privately acknowledging the forceful impact of those firm, straight shoulders under the soft material of his shirt, the undeniable attraction of a narrow waist and hips and those long, long legs, and a faintly rueful smile crossed her face at the memory of her original image of how she had expected Danny's father might look.

But *was* he Danny's father? The question about his wife had provoked a violent reaction, but that could simply mean that Luke and his wife had separated, he hadn't actually said that she was dead. She'd taken a risk asking that question, she thought on a sudden shiver of delayed reaction at the thought of her own temerity. Simply talking to Luke was like negotiating a minefield, never being sure when something might blow up right in her face. But when she'd asked it she'd been so *sure*, now doubt was beginning to creep back. For one thing, she could think of no possible rational reason why Luke should want to conceal his identity from her.

'Your drink.'

It took a determined effort of self-control not to reveal how his quiet words had startled her, intruding so unexpectedly on her thoughts. When had he turned? And had he caught her staring at him so unguardedly?

'Oh—thanks.' Her voice might have been a little uneven, but the hand that reached out for the glass was as steady as she could have wished, and it was as Luke picked up his own drink that she noticed the tautness of the muscles in his jaw, a betraying whiteness of the knuckles of the hand that held his whisky glass just a little too tightly.

So he wasn't quite as much in control as that swift switch to polite sociability had made him seem. Privately, Jill welcomed these tiny signs of Luke's inner unease, the tiny chinks in his seemingly impregnable armour; they made him seem so much more human. Perhaps he realised his cover had been blown, or perhaps——Her conscience pricked her sharply. If he *was* Garrett, then to ask about his wife had been a bit below the belt.

'I understand you can drive,' Luke said now, and anything he might have been feeling was once more carefully masked under a veneer of polite conversation, making Jill reject the uneasy guilty pang that had surfaced so unexpectedly. She was in grave danger of being a little too soft, crediting him with feelings he probably didn't possess. And after all, he was the one who'd put her in this quandary by not explaining to her exactly who he was.

'That's right, I passed my test before I went to college.'

Luke was feeling in his pocket for something. 'Here.'

He tossed her a bunch of keys which she caught awkwardly in her left hand.

'You'll need to transport Danny about a bit, I expect,

so the car's yours while you're here. Oh, not the Mercedes,' he added, reading the expression in Jill's eyes. 'There's a Fiat in the garage—that's yours. You can use it for private journeys too, provided you don't head for London every day off. The garage in Sorley will fill it up when it's needed and charge it to the account.'

'That's very generous——' Jill began, but as she hesitated, not knowing whether to add 'of you' or not, Luke continued as if she hadn't spoken.

'There are the keys to the house on there too—and one for the gate through to the swimming pool.' He had come close to her as she examined the keys and now he took them from her to identify the individual keys. 'Front door, back—swimming pool, car——' He shot her a swift unreadable glance, making her wonder if he had sensed her sudden tension. 'And this one will lock your bedroom door if you feel it's necessary,' he finished on a faintly ironical note. He dropped the keys back into her still outstretched palm with an abrupt movement. 'Any problems?'

'None I can think of.'

'Good.' Luke moved to sit in one of the armchairs. 'If anything crops up when Anne's not here I'm sure Jenky will put you right, especially if it's something to do with Danny. She knows him as well as anyone.'

There he went again! Ask Anne, ask Jenky—but don't bother *me*! Though of course that was fair enough if, as Garrett, he was likely to be away in London most of the time—or was he? He certainly seemed to regard himself as Garrett's spokesman on everything, and Jenky had included him in the 'family'—— Oh, stop it! Jill told herself firmly. Really, this analysis of everything the man said was way over the top!

She was just taking a much-needed sip at her sherry when she realised how closely Luke was watching her, his dark eyes suddenly so watchful and probing that she shifted uneasily where she stood as if the force of his gaze had actually brushed against a vulnerable nerve. His forehead was creased in a thoughtful frown, and her uneasiness grew as she wondered just what it was that had brought that dark expression to his face.

She knew what he was seeing, a slim girl, medium height, with golden-blonde hair cut in a short, smooth bob, a heart-shaped face, tilted nose and small, full mouth. Her eyes were her best feature; of a soft blue-green, they had once been likened to aquamarines by a poetically inclined boyfriend at college, but right now she felt she would willingly trade them for a few curves in the right places or a wave or two in her uncompromisingly straight hair. She was well aware of the fact that, in spite of the extra effort she had made tonight, adding eyeshadow and blusher to her usual touch of mascara and hint of lipstick, nothing ever seemed to make her look her age. She knew she looked young and unsophisticated, and that put her at a distinct disadvantage where Luke was concerned. His own worldliness was stamped all over him, etched into the lines on his face, and she had no desire to appear naïve in his eyes.

'Come and sit down. Dinner won't be ready for ten minutes or so, and there's something I want to ask you.'

Luke's voice was quiet enough, though she wouldn't go so far as to describe it as friendly, but his face had lost none of that frowning watchfulness, and although she did as he asked with every appearance of calm she was unable to prevent her stomach from clenching painfully in apprehension. Just what had put that look on his face?

He had put down his drink and was reaching for his cigarettes. With the packet in his hand he turned that searching dark blue gaze on her once more.

'What would you do if someone offered you money— a lot of money—for information about Danny?' he asked suddenly.

The question came so unexpectedly that for a moment Jill could only stare at him, shocked and bewildered. She couldn't quite believe that she'd heard him correctly and she found herself unable to look away from the dark eyes that were fixed on her face, holding hers with mesmeric force, watching her intently as she struggled to find the words to answer him.

'But they wouldn't would they——? I mean, no one—— Who would want to?'

Luke inclined his head slightly to one side. 'There are some who might,' he said calmly enough, but, hypersensitive to the hard edge to his voice, Jill felt a sensation like the trickle of icy water run down her spine making her feel suddenly shiveringly cold. 'The press, for example.'

'But why?'

He paused to light his cigarette before replying, deliberately drawing out the moment, Jill was sure, his eyes never leaving her pale, anxious face.

'Garrett is a very wealthy man and pretty well known, down south at least. There are plenty of people who feel that what he or his family does is news.'

There was more than an edge to his voice now and the way he sat forward in his seat, every muscle tense like those of a hunting cat crouched ready to spring, made her think uneasily of the interrogation scenes in all the spy films she had ever seen. Nervously she stirred in her chair, not knowing what to say, but then the full force of what Luke was implying struck home with the force of a bullet and she lifted her chin defiantly, her eyes flashing sea-green fire.

'And you think that *I* would sell them information! How *dare* you! How could you even *think*——'

She broke off abruptly, struggling with the sense of outrage that was filling her. There was no response to her outburst from the man opposite, but she knew he had noted every fleeting expression that crossed her face. His eyes were so sharply probing that she felt they might actually pierce her skin where his gaze landed.

'You can't believe I would!' she cried at last, a note of desperation in her voice.

'You said money was tight at home,' Luke put in ominously quietly.

'Well, so it is!' Jill exploded furiously. 'But not so damn tight that I'd stoop to what you're suggesting to improve things! What sort of an unfeeling monster do you think I am?'

Then, because once again her emotions threatened to overwhelm her, she bit her lip hard, clenching her hands tightly into fists in an effort to regain control. In a way, Luke's silent, impassive scrutiny disturbed her far more than the things he had said. It was the way a fox watched a rabbit just before it pounced, and it frightened her. She felt instinctively that this man had the power to hurt her if he chose, hurt her in a way no one else had ever been able to, though she didn't quite know why. It wasn't that she was totally inexperienced where men were concerned, there had been plenty of light-hearted relationships during her time at college, but nothing had prepared her for dealing with a man like Luke. He was pure tiger and beside him all the boys she had known would look like cuddly pussycats.

With an effort she pulled herself together. It wouldn't do to let Luke see the effect he had on her.

'Have you finished?' she demanded in a low, angry voice. 'Or is there anything else you'd like to know—my criminal record, perhaps?'

One corner of the straight, hard mouth curled upwards briefly, so briefly that she could never have called Luke's reaction a smile, but at least it was a response. He moved then, reaching for his glass and draining it before crossing the room to the drinks cabinet.

'It was a question that had to be asked,' he said calmly. 'More sherry?'

Jill could only shake her head, too drained by the

powerful emotions that had swept through her to speak.
Luke stood for a moment, looking into her face with a
thoughtful expression in his narrowed eyes, but this
time there was a new and almost gentle light in their
sombre depths.

'You're a real innocent, aren't you?' he murmured
slowly. 'It had really never occurred to you that someone
might take this job for anything other than the obviously
admirable motives you have.'

Then, as she dropped her eyes to stare at the floor,
unsure of how to interpret that faintly ironical 'admirable' and completely at a loss as to how to react to this
strangely altered Luke, he went on almost kindly,
'Don't take it so personally. I would have had to ask
anyone else the same question—surely you can see that?'

'Yes—yes, I can.'

Nervously Jill smoothed the blue and white cotton of
her skirt, embarrassed by the way her voice had
trembled as she spoke. She felt out of her depth,
suddenly caught up in a world in which the intrusion of
the press was part of life, something to be lived with.
Clearly this was why Garrett guarded his privacy with
such excessive zeal.

The movement of her hand suddenly stilled as
another thought struck her. In her shock at Luke's
unexpected and disturbing question she had temporarily
forgotten her suspicions that he and Garrett were one
and the same person; now that puzzle came flooding
back into her mind, but she found she was viewing it in a
new and very different light. She felt she had taken a step
towards understanding why he might feel it necessary to
resort to the subterfuge of not telling her who he was.

'Danny must know nothing of this,' Luke's sharp
voice broke into her thoughts, bringing her head up
swiftly.

'Of course not! You can trust me!'

She met his eyes unflinchingly as she spoke, sincerity

ringing clearly in her voice, and surprisingly, in spite of
the fact that his gaze was as direct and keen as before, she
didn't find the experience quite so unnerving as she had
earlier, or rather, it was disturbing in a completely
different way. There was something new in the
midnight-blue depths, something that had never been
there before. She wouldn't go so far as to describe it as
warmth, rather it was a lightening of the darkness.

'Yes,' Luke said slowly, 'I rather think I can.'

Dinner was a rather silent meal, Luke seeming to have
become absorbed in some private thoughts of his own,
but Jill refused to let this fact inhibit her as, having
discovered that she was ravenously hungry, she tackled
the soup and chicken salad with enthusiasm and
appreciation. She shook her head when Luke offered to
pour her some wine, indicating the scarcely-touched
glass of sherry she had brought to the table.

'I'll stick to this, if you don't mind. I'm afraid I've no
head for alcohol, so I'd better not risk it.'

It was as she lifted the last spoonful of a wonderful
apple pie to her mouth that Luke, who had refused the
dessert himself, stirred at last, reaching for the wine to
refill his glass.

'Where do you put it all?' he asked lazily. 'You're such
a little thing, after all.'

To her consternation Jill felt warm colour flood her
cheeks at the thought that he had been watching her. So
much for trying not to appear unsophisticated!

'I——' she began hastily, but Luke raised one hand to
silence her, his heavy-lidded eyes glinting with unconcealed amusement.

'I didn't mean to embarrass you—and Jenky will be
pleased that someone appreciates her cooking. She quite
despairs of me.' He pushed the pie towards Jill. 'There's
plenty more—help yourself.'

'Oh no.' She leaned back in her chair, relaxing in the
sudden lessening of tension between them. 'Even I have

my limits. I couldn't eat another thing!' she laughed, and then froze in astonishment as Luke grinned in response, the sudden, unexpected smile transforming his face, smoothing out the harsh lines and lighting his eyes with a genuine warmth.

'Coffee, then?'

'Mmm.' Her response was abstracted, her mind busy on other things. Just for a moment she had seen another side of Luke, a lazy, good-humoured charm that she was willing to bet most women would find devastating, and that smile would melt a far harder heart than her own—but she'd be crazy if she let herself fall for it! Her appreciation of the sudden change was reduced to a purely objective acknowledgement, that charming smile failing to have the desired effect because in the moment Luke's face had changed so completely she had suddenly known, once and for all, without any doubts, just who he was. Disregarding such matters as the differences in colouring, age and size, when that dancing laughter lit his eyes from within it had been Danny's face she had seen opposite her, his mischievous expression mirrored exactly in his father's.

For a split second she knew a tormenting desire to lift her hand and slap that smile from Luke's face, wanting to express as forcefully as she could the anger she felt. How dared he deceive her like this, playing some crazy game with her for his own private reasons! Then as the flare of temper waned and rational thought returned she allowed herself a secret, inward smile at the realisation that there was a much better way to pay him back. Two could play at this game! If he could pretend to be someone else then she could make believe as well, letting him think she believed his subterfuge. Impulsively she leaned forward.

'Can I ask you something?' Her voice sounded satisfactorily innocent and she was sure he suspected nothing as he nodded his answer. 'It's about Mr

Garrett.' She used the name carefully, almost as
carefully as she now realised he had always used it, so
that she could almost hear the quotation marks around
the words, and watching his reaction closely she saw the
smile fade and the warmth leave his eyes as mentally he
took several steps away from her.

'You never give up, do you?' he said discouragingly.

'But it's not just him——' Seeing the cold, shuttered
mask slide back over Luke's face, Jill almost lost her
nerve—but she'd started now, and she couldn't just
blurt out that she knew who he was. 'It's about Danny
too.'

Luke's sigh was a sound of barely controlled
impatience.

'Just what are you trying to say?'

'Well——' Jill took a deep breath and brought the
words out in a rush. 'It's just that if Mr Garrett is as
wealthy as you say then surely he doesn't have to be
away *all* the time. Hasn't he made enough money for
anyone?' Her voice strengthened, gathered conviction
because now she was talking about something she felt
very strongly, and in a strange way it was easier to talk
about it from behind the shelter of the pretence that
Luke was not Garrett, easier to use that impersonal 'he'
instead of the direct and much more sensitive 'you'.
'Can't he see how much Danny needs him—all the more
so if what you've said about the press is true—that isn't
exactly a *normal* way to live, is it? I just don't see how he
can leave Danny alone as much as he does.'

'Danny has his grandmother.' That note of warning
was creeping into Luke's voice once more, erasing the
softer tones, making it ominously hard and cold so that
Jill's stomach clenched fearfully at the sound. She'd
caught him on the raw there!

'But that's not enough! At least, I don't think it is.
What sort of man is Garrett if he puts his business
interests before his son's happiness?'

This was like some crazy game of mental chess, with each of them hiding their thoughts from the other, making careful oblique moves that they hoped would disguise what they were doing but would eventually bring them to their final goal—though what Luke's goal was she really had no idea.

'A business doesn't run itself.' His tone was definitely dangerous now, but Jill was too involved to notice. She'd almost forgotten exactly why she'd started out on this in the first place, her idea of revenge obscured by a deep-felt need to help Danny in any way she could.

'That's no defence! You said yourself that Garrett wasn't here as much as Danny needed him to be. Surely there must be other people who can run things in London so that y——' she caught herself up sharply, feeling a quiver of alarm at how close she had come to giving herself away, '*he* can spend more time at home! If he had to banish Danny up here then the least he could do is to arrange things so that he could see him more often or——' *Could* she say it? Oh well, she might as well be hanged for a sheep as a lamb. 'Or he could have married again, had other——'

'I think you've said enough!'

The fury in Luke's voice brought her up sharp, making her look at him properly for the first time since she had launched into that last, impetuous speech. His face was set and hard, his skin stretched tight over the strong bones, showing white at nose and mouth and his eyes were just blue chips of ice.

'I——' she began, then stopped as her voice failed her completely.

'You have made your opinions quite clear, Miss Carpenter.' Jill winced mentally as she felt the impact of those freezingly precise words. 'But as I've told you before, you are employed here for a short time to look after Daniel, nothing more, and I would be obliged if you would keep to that arrangement, whatever your personal feelings.' The last two words were given a distinctly scathing emphasis. 'If you don't like the situation you can leave right now—just pack your bags and go. But if you do decide to stay you'd better learn to curb that over-active tongue of yours, because, believe me, a pretty face and wide baby-blue eyes don't deceive me for one minute. You, lady, are trouble with a capital T. I knew that from the moment I saw you.'

That 'over-active tongue' was sorely tempted to tell Luke to go to hell and stay there, taking his job, his obsessions and this whole crazy pretence with him. Jill's lips had even opened to fling the angry retort in his face when her brain registered just what he had said after that, and the words dried in her throat. *Pretty*? Had he really said pretty?

'And while we're putting our cards on the table,' he continued in the ruthlessly controlled voice Jill was already coming to dread, 'there's one other thing you ought to know——'

Oh lord, no, not now! she exclaimed inwardly, knowing only too well what was coming and that it couldn't have happened at a worse moment.

'I'm afraid I haven't been completely honest with you, Miss Carpenter,' Luke was saying, and the cold condescension of his tone, the stiff formality of her name, grated on nerves already raw after the trials and tensions of the day, combining with the anger that lingered just below the surface of her mind with the force of an explosion, making her forget all other considerations beyond the fact that she had been deliberately and cold-bloodedly deceived. Deciding that attack was the best form of defence, she gave him no chance to continue.

'No, you haven't been honest with me!' she cried vehemently. 'In fact you've lied to me from the moment I met you. And if you're thinking of coming clean now, then I have to tell you that you're too damn late, *Mr*

*Garrett*! I'm not quite the fool you took me for—I've got eyes, I can see—and anyone who wasn't completely blind would be able to tell that Danny is your son!'

Her outburst didn't have quite the effect she had anticipated. One tiny flicker of a glance at her indignant face was the only response Luke made, after that he sat still and silent, remote as a statue carved in marble. Then as the sound of her angry words died away his expression changed and she could only stare in frank incredulity as the corners of his mouth curled into a slow smile.

'Well, now I think we understand each other,' he said, getting to his feet. 'I apologise for having deceived you in this way, but I can assure you that I had very good reasons for doing so.' Once more he turned that disturbingly direct dark blue gaze on her. 'But let me put you straight on something—whatever else I may think of you, the one thing I never took you for was a fool.'

He had gone before she could even begin to think of a reply. For a long time she stayed where she was, sitting at the table, staring at the door that Luke had closed so firmly behind him, his last words repeating over and over in her head. She found it hard to believe she had heard him right, and her consternation was only increased by the belated realisation that the slow, sardonic smile that had curved his mouth had, incredibly, been one of rather cynical appreciation.

# CHAPTER FOUR

'COME IN.'

Luke's curt command from the other side of the study door did nothing to restore Jill's confidence, which had been slowly seeping away in the seconds since she had knocked.

She had had no direct contact with Luke since the previous night, he had hidden himself in his study all day, only emerging when Danny and Mrs Logan had returned to Stoneroyd. But now Danny was in bed, his grandmother had left for the airport, and she had been summoned to Luke's study to receive her final instructions before his own departure the following morning. The prospect of facing him like this made her shiver as she recalled how she had spoken to him yesterday. How could she have let her tongue run away with her like that?

No! She pulled herself together as Luke's command to enter was repeated, more impatiently this time. She had said things she felt needed saying, and she still felt the same way now, even if it did make things so very difficult between herself and her employer. All the same, remembering the look on his face, she could wish she'd never opened her mouth. Taking a deep breath, she went into the room.

Luke was at his desk, writing busily. He glanced up as she came in and indicated a chair with a wave of his hand.

'Sit down, Miss Carpenter. I'll be with you in a minute.'

Watching him as he became absorbed in his work once more, the glow from the desk lamp that was the only light in the room illuminating the strong lines of his face, the tightness about his mouth and jaw, Jill couldn't help recalling how, with Danny, Luke's face had changed so dramatically. Those same harsh lines had softened, the normally severe mouth had shown that it could smile, and the cold eyes had gleamed with amusement as he listened to his son's account of his two days away and watched the artful showing off the child had indulged in for Jill's benefit.

At one moment, seeing him like that, catching him unaware that she was watching, she had suddenly realised that, contrary to her first impression of him, he was in fact an extremely attractive man, and having once seen that she was forced to wonder how she could ever have thought him not particularly handsome before.

Not an easy face to get to know, Jill decided, but one that repaid close consideration with something much more satisfying than the bland description 'good-looking'. And what about the mind behind that face? Would that too reward the effort of time and patience needed to understand it with a strength of personality that she suspected would make all other men she had ever known pale into insignificance? From some previously unconsidered part of her mind came a sudden surge of longing to find out, stunning her with a force of impact that made her head reel and sending a rush of blood to her face.

'I'm sorry to keep you waiting.'

Luke signed the letter he had been writing and looked up. As his eyes turned in her direction she was suddenly very glad of the deepening shadows of dusk as she was overwhelmed by the irrational feeling that he could tell exactly what she had been thinking, and she was thankful that the gathering darkness hid the colour of her cheeks. He straightened the papers before him then paused, his expression thoughtful, the fingers of his right hand twisting his wedding ring round and round.

'I can understand that you feel angry at the way I deceived you,' he said at last, his tone pitched at a level of careful politeness, 'but I hope you will appreciate that I felt it was necessary. As I told you earlier, I cannot take risks where Danny is concerned. I had to know that you could be trusted.'

'And what would you have done if you'd felt I couldn't?' Caught between acknowledging that she did understand and the smart of the anger she had felt at Luke's subterfuge, Jill found it impossible to prevent her voice from sounding tight and stiff, her tension in no way eased by his acknowledgement of her feelings.

'You would have been on the first bus back home and we would have found someone else.' She was subjected to another of those disturbingly direct glances. 'There were other applicants.'

'And now?'

He inclined his head consideringly. 'Anne is convinced that you can do the job very well, and having seen you with Danny I think you can too.'

'So I can stay?' Try as she might, she couldn't control the quaver of relief in her voice, and evidently Luke caught it too, his brows jerking together in surprise as his eyes narrowed swiftly.

'Yes, Miss Carpenter, you can stay.'

Jill was frankly stunned by the powerful sense of release that swept through her, the sudden relaxation of muscles she hadn't been aware of having held taut telling her how important Luke's decision was to her.

'Thank you,' she said quietly, earning herself another of those searching glances from his heavy-lidded blue eyes.

'Perhaps we should be the ones thanking you for being prepared to stay,' he said cryptically. 'Well, we shall see. Now,' his tone changed, becoming crisp and business-like, 'you'll need some money for everyday expenses.'

He reached for an envelope that lay on his desk and held it out to her.

'This should cover the next fortnight or so until I get back on the twenty-seventh, but if it doesn't Jenky will give you some more out of the housekeeping account. I don't want you to be out of pocket while you're with us.'

The brown envelope was unsealed, and Jill could not suppress a gasp of surprise at the sight of the amount of money it contained.

'I'm sure this will be more than enough. I'll keep a record of how I spend it.'

One corner of Luke's mouth quirked up into his strange half-smile. 'Your scrupulous honesty does you credit, but I don't think that will be necessary,' he said, the note of irony in his voice making her prickle with irritation. 'I'm sure you'll spend the money wisely. Just use it to make Danny happy, that's all I ask.'

And having provided the cash, he thought he'd fulfilled his role as a father! Jill thought angrily. Did he think that was *all* Danny needed to make him happy? To her horror, Luke's sudden frown told her she had recklessly spoken her thoughts out loud.

'Miss Carpenter, I wish you would rid yourself of the delusion that you are my moral counsellor.' The sardonic voice sliced through the air like a cold steel blade. 'I thought I'd already made it plain that your interference is not appreciated.'

'Interference' stung as it was clearly intended to. 'I'm not taking back a word I said,' she declared stiffly.

Luke's sigh was drily resigned. 'I never expected you would. Tell me, do you attack everyone in this way, or is this a purely personal vendetta?'

The satirical question threw her completely.

'I—no——' she floundered, biting her lip in confusion. Luke's closed and shuttered expression offered her no help or encouragement and she would have been a fool to expect any. 'I——' she tried again, then in the

whirl of disturbed feelings in her mind one thought
emerged clear and sharp. 'I didn't know who you were at
first!' she protested unevenly, privately very shaken by
the discovery of just how much his deception had hurt.

'No, you didn't,' Luke conceded. 'Are you trying to
tell me you wouldn't have said anything if you'd
known?'

*Would* she? She'd said she didn't retract anything and
she'd meant it.

'I would have been more—tactful,' she managed
stiffly, meeting those searching blue eyes deliberately
and with a hint of defiance that she hoped would hide
the nervousness twisting her stomach muscles into
knots. Only minutes after Luke had agreed to let her stay
she was risking her job with every word she spoke. She
wanted this job, was frankly stunned to realise just how
much she wanted it, but she wasn't going to lie to get it.

For a long, taut moment dark eyes locked with lighter
ones, Luke's face unsmiling as ever, but then, incredu-
lously, Jill thought she saw something close to respect
glimmering like a faint candle flame in the navy blue
depths. For a second she felt intuitively that he was
seeing her very differently, seeing her as something
other than the infuriatingly persistent critic he had
previously considered her to be. Then, abruptly, he
broke the fragile contact, glancing down at his watch,
and she could almost feel him taking a mental step
backwards away from her. The next moment it was as if
that undefinable second had never been as he changed
the subject deliberately.

'Don't let Danny run rings round you, Miss Carpenter. He's a lovable little rogue, but he knows perfectly
well how to charm people into giving him just what he
wants, and I don't want him spoiled.' Another of those
disconcertingly direct glances accompanied Luke's
words. 'We may have plenty of money, but I don't want
him to think that's all there is in life.'

Jill knew her thoughts must show on her face, but there was nothing she could do about it. With an effort she squashed them down. She had only just avoided serious trouble after letting her tongue run wild; another outburst would be more than Luke could tolerate. The faint smile hovering around those firm, straight lips told her that he was very much aware of the struggle she was having to keep quiet.

'So,' he went on, 'I would appreciate it if you could encourage him in activities that any child, without his privileges, would enjoy. Knowing your opinions, I'm sure you'll understand what I mean.'

She winced inwardly at the cynical edge to that comment.

Why did he have to squash her like that? Jill wondered, the too-familiar irritation pricking at her again. What was it about herself and this man that they seemed unable to talk to each other without hostility coming between them?

'I've left my London phone number here,' Luke indicated the pad beside the telephone, 'in case of emergency.' Once more she was subjected to that disturbing intense scrutiny.

'And if there is an emergency I want to know—but I don't want to be troubled over small things.'

'I'm not one to panic unnecessarily.' It was impossible to keep the tartness out of her voice. 'And I'll do my best not to *interfere* with your private arrangements.'

She hadn't been able to resist the emphasis on the word he had used so scathingly to her a short time earlier, and she felt a small surge of satisfaction at seeing the way his hand tightened on the pen he had picked up.

'If I could be sure you would keep to that,' Luke drawled silkily, 'then I think life would be a great deal easier for everyone.'

The sound of her bedroom door opening brought Jill

awake with a start. As she raised herself on one elbow a small figure came to stand by the bed.

'My daddy's gone,' Danny announced in mournful tones. 'The house is all empty and I'm too sad to sleep.'

Through sleep-blurred eyes she surveyed the little boy's stiffly rigid face that warred with the wide, tear-filled eyes and trembling bottom lip, and felt a rush of sympathy for him. Her clock told her that it was still only six; clearly Luke had lost no time in departing for London.

'Come on, poppet,' she said gently. 'Snuggle in with me and we'll have a cuddle.'

As the tense little body moved close up to her she put her arms round him and held him tightly. How could he! she thought angrily. How *could* Luke leave Danny alone so often!

'I wanted my daddy to stay,' Danny said, his head on her shoulder.

'Sometimes daddys have to go to work, pet,' Jill murmured softly, trying to inject a conviction she wasn't feeling into the words.

'But I *wanted* him to stay,' Danny repeated forlornly. He raised his head slightly to look into her face. 'Will you stay, Auntie Jill?'

'Of course I'll stay.' This time there was no problem in making the words sound sincere. 'That's why I've come, to look after you. We'll have a lovely time together. We can have walks and picnics and go swimming——'

'And have ice-creams,' Danny suggested, sounding more cheerful.

'Yes, and have ice-creams,' laughed Jill.

Gradually she felt the child relax against her. Perhaps he would sleep now—and when he woke, she promised herself, things would be different. For the short time she was with him at least, Danny would not be lonely, not if she could help it.

'Daddy said I was to be good,' Danny muttered drowsily. 'But I wanted my daddy to stay.' His voice trailed off and he slept.

Jill lay awake beside him, her mind full of plans for their time together, but underneath all her ideas for the activities they would share she was disturbed to find an inexplicable emptiness, a small sore spot in her mind like a bruise that ached when she tried to probe the reasons for its existence. She couldn't understand why it was there, lying at the bottom of her mind like a jagged rock below the water's surface, ready to trap the unwary sailor and tear a hole in the boat he had previously thought so safe. She wasn't homesick, her time at college had cured her of any such feelings, she wasn't missing her flatmates, theirs was the sort of friendship that could stand long periods apart, keeping in touch by letter and taking up from the point at which they had left off when they finally met up again. There was no love of her life from whom she had parted at the end of her course. She had had some very happy relationships with several male students, all of whom had remained friends when the romantic attachment had died, but none of them had been anything more serious than a gentle caring, she had not yet met that special man to whom she could give the love and commitment that would mean their absence would cause anything more than a mild regret. So why did she feel lost and bereft as if something very important had gone out of her life?

It was only when her thoughts wandered to the image of the silver-grey Mercedes with Luke inside it, already well on his way to London, that the truth hit her with a force that caused her heart to miss a beat. In two short days, irritating and disturbing as he was, Luke had become so much a part of her life at Stoneroyd that, like Danny, she found that just the thought of his absence made the house 'all empty', and as she lay there watching the rays of sunlight stretch themselves across the carpet she knew that she too was too sad to sleep.

'Goodnight, Danny. Sleep well.'

Jill closed the bedroom door and wandered into the nursery, but found herself unable to settle to anything. The evening was cool and fresh, there was nothing on television she wanted to watch and Jenky had gone out to visit some friends in Sorley, depriving her of the cheerful companionship the two women had shared most evenings in the past ten days. She felt restless; ideally she would have liked to go outside for a walk, but her responsibilities to Danny meant that she had to stay within earshot of his call.

Danny. A smile crossed Jill's face at the thought of the little boy now tucked up safely in bed. He seemed so much more relaxed these days, revelling in the change from the rather rigid, organised way of life he had lived with his grandmother. The two of them now shared breakfast in the big, sunny kitchen, chatting to Jenky as they ate. Lunch was eaten outside whenever possible and, as the weather stayed fine and dry, that meant a picnic most days either sprawled on a rug on the lawn or in the countryside when they went out in the car. Jill also joined Danny at teatime, thankful that she did not have to eat in solitary splendour in the dining-room, and these nursery teas after a long, active day in the sun and with the prospect of a long bath and bedtime story ahead of them had soon become her favourite time of day.

The new way of life suited Danny. He loved the freedom and activity and soon developed a healthy tan and an even healthier appetite. Worn out as he was at the end of each day, there was never any trouble in getting him to sleep, and, although he mentioned Luke every day, saying wistfully that he wished his daddy was home, Jill was glad to see that he never returned to the forlorn despondency of that first morning.

She picked up a book but could not concentrate on the

plot. Restlessly she flung it down. She would get herself a drink; perhaps that would help her to relax.

In the garden room she poured herself a sherry and was about to take a sip from it when the tape deck caught her eye. Ever since she had first played the cassette, when Luke had come in and stopped her, she had wanted to hear more of it, to try to recall just what memories it evoked.

'No one will know.' She spoke the words out loud, they seemed more convincing that way. 'There's no one here to see.'

The cassette was still in the machine, no one had touched it since the night Luke had switched it off so abruptly. With the memory of that night so clear in her mind, Jill couldn't suppress the urge to cast an involuntary glance over her shoulder as she pressed the 'play' button as if she expected he might suddenly appear as he had done that night.

But from the moment she heard the first note of music all other thoughts were forgotten as she listened, entranced as she had been that first time. The memories she was trying to recapture still eluded her, obscured by the mists of time, but that no longer seemed to matter as she sat in the darkening room, her untouched drink in her hand, absorbed in the music and the words. Unbidden, thoughts of Luke rose up her mind, the hard, unapproachable man she had first met, and the gentler, more relaxed person she had seen him become so briefly in the company of his young son.

Why had he been so adamant that the records and cassettes were not to be touched? A faint frown creased Jill's forehead as she considered the contradiction between Luke's work in London and his home life at Stoneroyd. He had said that his job involved music recording and publishing, and yet, accustomed as she was to the way her flatmates at college and her mother at home always had the radio or a record playing, she thought she had never lived anywhere quite as silent as the big old house. She had also been stunned to discover just how few children's songs Danny knew, never singing to himself as he played as her nieces almost invariably did, and had set herself to rectify the lack in his life. The little boy's response had been immediate and enthusiastic. Like someone who has just discovered the reason for his existence, he had set himself to learning the simple tunes she had taught him, revealing a strong, clear voice and an amazing ability to carry a melody in his head, and she had been hard put to meet his persistent demands for 'a new song, Auntie Jill' which stretched her knowledge to its limits.

It was as the last notes on the tape died away that she heard the sound of a car's wheels on the gravel outside. Strong headlights shone through the window, bringing her to her feet in a rush. Jenky must have come back earlier than she had planned; it wouldn't do to be caught playing the tapes that Luke had expressly forbidden her to touch. She was moving towards the machine to switch it off when a thin, high-pitched scream reached her from upstairs, freezing her to the spot.

'Daddy!'

Another scream echoed through the silent house, jolting Jill into action as, forgetting everything else, she dashed upstairs.

'*Daddy*! Daddy! Help me!' Danny's panic-stricken voice sounded clearly as she reached the landing and flung open the bedroom door.

He was sitting up in bed, staring wide-eyed and terrified at the sudden light, one hand clutching at what bedclothes remained with him, most of them lying in a bundle on the floor.

'Danny—what is it, sweetheart?'

But Danny just stared straight through her as if he did not recognise her. 'There's crocodiles in my bed!' he shrieked.

Jill relaxed immediately. A nightmare, that was all. From his screams she had feared something far worse.

'It's all right, pet, it was just a dream. Auntie Jill's here now, we'll have a cuddle and it will all go away.'

She moved towards the bed, intending to take him in her arms, but to her horror he screamed again and cowered away from her.

'No! I want my daddy!'

Vaguely Jill noted the sound of footsteps on the stairs. Jenky was coming, perhaps she would be able to help. Somehow they had to calm Danny before he worked himself up any more. She turned thankfully towards the open door, glad of Jenky's comfortable, dependable presence.

'He's had a nightmare, Jenky—but he won't let me touch him. Can you——'

The words died on her lips when she saw the tall figure in the doorway. Not Jenky but Luke, a tired, strained-looking Luke who nevertheless seemed to take in the situation in a glance. Jill saw his eyes go straight to Danny, saw the flash of some powerful and very raw emotion in their navy blue depths before, ignoring her completely, he moved to gather the frightened child to him.

'It's all right, little man, Daddy's here.'

Luke's voice was infinitely gentle, the strong arms encircled the trembling body, one long-fingered hand caressing the child's dark hair. The scene before her was so unlike the sort of behaviour she had come to expect from Luke that she found herself unable to drag her eyes away, holding her breath for fear of destroying the moment.

'Daddy,' Danny's voice was muffled as his face was pressed tight up against Luke's chest, 'Daddy, there's crocodiles in my bed, big fierce crocodiles.'

Briefly Jill wondered what Luke would make of that, half suspecting that he would tell Danny not to be so silly—and then rejecting the idea in the same instant, she wasn't at all sure how this new Luke would react. In the end it came as no real surprise when, gently disengaging himself from the little boy's clutching fingers, Luke lifted the blankets from the tumbled heap on the floor.

'That rotten old crocodile again, is it? Well, we know what to do with him—got you!'

Bending down, he pretended to grab something by the scruff of the neck, then, completely unself-consciously, still carrying the imaginary crocodile, he crossed to the window, opened it and tossed the creature out. Then he returned to Danny and pulled the little boy on to his knee.

'There now, little man, I've put him out the window. He's gone—look!'

He lifted the bedclothes to prove that they were indeed free from crocodiles. By now Danny's sobs had subsided to a series of loud sniffs.

'He was *big* an' fierce.'

'Yes, he was,' Luke agreed. 'But he's gone now. Minstrel and Tara'll deal with him—that's what they're here for, they're guard dogs, aren't they?' With a gentle hand he wiped the damp tearstains from his son's face. 'Now, would you like a drink, then I'll sing you some songs if you promise to cuddle up and go to sleep. Do you want some milk?'

Danny nodded drowsily. Now fully relaxed, leaning against his father's chest, he looked half asleep already.

'Will you sing the sleepytown song?'

Luke laughed, a soft, happy sound that made Jill's breath catch in her throat. With the memory of her own thoughts of Luke earlier that evening still in her mind, making her hypersensitive to the change in her employer, she found this new Luke infinitely more disturbing than the cold, indifferent man she was used to seeing.

'All right,' Luke was saying, 'the sleepytown song.

But have that drink first.'

'I'll fetch it,' offered Jill, making Luke glance at her for the first time since he had come into the room. For a moment he seemed taken aback as if only just becoming aware of her presence, then he nodded silently and turned his attention back to Danny.

'We'd better get this bed sorted out.'

In the nursery, Jill went through the motions of finding a cup and filling it purely automatically as she struggled to collect her whirling thoughts. Where had Luke suddenly appeared from—and why had he come? He wasn't due back for almost another week, and yet here he was, luckily just when she needed him. Her conscience pricked her sharply at the thought of the accusations of heartlessness she had flung at him, she knew instinctively that she could never have calmed Danny so quickly—or dealt with the crocodile so efficiently, she thought on a smile—without him.

But what had brought him back to Stoneroyd so unexpectedly? She had to admit she didn't know, but she could only be grateful that the tape she had been playing had finished before he had entered the house or he would have caught her in the act of disobeying his orders that the stereo was not to be touched.

When she took the milk into the bedroom Danny was back in bed, looking as if he could barely keep his eyes open. Luke took the cup from her hand, held it while Danny gulped down his drink, then, still without a word, handed it back to Jill. Once more she noted how tired and drawn he looked.

'I'll have some coffee ready for you when you've finished,' she said quietly.

'Thanks.' Luke's response was brief to the point of curtness, his attention only on his son.

On the landing Jill paused for a moment to pull the door to behind her. Inside the room she heard Luke begin to sing a lullaby and the sound kept her standing

where she was, unable to move because of the shock that
paralysed her. The tune was just a simple children's
melody, the words nothing more than a string of
rhyming nonsense, but the voice held her spellbound
because she had heard it before, and heard it less than
half an hour earlier. Huskily attractive, sensual and yet
hauntingly gentle, it had been *Luke's* voice she had
heard on the tape.

# CHAPTER FIVE

'THIS is yours, I believe, unless Jenky has taken to tippling sherry in the evenings.'

Jill caught her breath, staring in consternation at the glass Luke held out to her. It contained the sherry she had poured herself earlier and, remembering where she had left it, knowing she had left the cassette player switched on, she didn't dare to meet Luke's eyes, afraid of what she might see there.

She had been pouring boiling water into a coffee mug when she had heard Danny's bedroom door open and Luke's footsteps going downstairs. Telling herself that she had never really expected that he would join her, in spite of her offer of coffee, she had refused even to acknowledge the wave of disappointment that swept through her at his abrupt departure and had determined to have this coffee anyway and then take herself off to bed. But Luke had only gone to get himself a glass of whisky, and she had barely seated herself in an armchair before he was back, carrying his own drink and her incriminating sherry glass with him.

'But as I met Jenky downstairs and she's only just got back from an evening out, I can only assume this yours.' There was nothing in his voice or expression to give her any clue as to what he was thinking, but it seemed the volcano wasn't about to erupt just yet, so she reached out and took the glass from him.

'Thanks. I—I'd just poured it when Danny screamed. I'd completely forgotten about it.'

'So it seems,' was the non-committal response, no hint of anything dangerous in either his voice or expression, so that Jill allowed herself to relax a little as

Luke lowered himself into the chair opposite her and took a sip from his own glass. He rubbed the back of his hand across his eyes in a tired gesture that made her study him more closely.

The pallor of his face was shocking, as was the heaviness of his eyes, the dark shadows of them giving them a faintly bruised look. Lines of weariness were etched around his nose and mouth, and seeing them Jill shifted uncomfortably in her seat as her conscience reproved her once more, her heart twisting painfully at the realisation that Luke was nowhere near as invulnerable as he had at first appeared. This was not the hard, untouchable man she had first met but another Luke, a very human man exhausted by the pressures of business and home.

'Have you driven up from London tonight?' she asked, and at his nod of agreement went on, 'We weren't expecting you.'

'I know. I came back on an impulse. Things took much less time than I had anticipated, so I thought I'd take a break, have a few days off. There was a final conference this afternoon, I left as soon as that had finished. There was nothing else I had to do and——' he shot Jill a sharp, testing glance and she caught the sudden flash of flame deep in his eyes, 'and certain comments made me feel that perhaps I'd better spend some time here.'

So he *had* listened to her! But it wasn't a completely comfortable realisation. Painfully aware of the fact that those comments had been made without a full awareness of the facts, Jill found it hard to keep her voice level as she asked, 'Does Danny have these nightmares often?'

'I've dealt with them before,' Luke said flatly, his expression suddenly bleak and desolate. 'Danny takes after his mother. Marianne—my wife—was always rather highly strung.'

The blank, emotionless voice was somehow shocking,

and something twisted sharply in her heart at the thought of a small incident that had brought the death of Luke's wife clearly into focus.

She had been helping Jenky to clean the study, the housekeeper snatching the opportunity afforded by Luke's absence to risk entering her employer's most private room, his bedroom being only somewhere he slept, something she would never dare do when he was actually at Stoneroyd. It was as she was replacing a pile of papers on the desk top that the picture had fallen to the floor.

Expecting as she was to see a likeness of Luke's wife, Jill was unprepared for the beauty of the woman before her. Even though the portrait was only a simple pencil sketch, the artist had been so skilled that the face looked vividly alive, almost as if it could speak. She saw the clear, wide eyes, high cheekbones and long, shining dark hair, and knew instinctively why Luke had never remarried. No one would ever be able to replace this woman in his heart.

There was a touch of sadness about the woman's mouth, almost as if she had known her life would not last long, and, remembering Danny's face on the morning Luke had left for London, Jill had felt she could begin to understand rather better just why Luke spent as much of his time away from home as he did. Danny was so like his mother that his presence must be a constant reminder to him of the woman he had loved and lost.

Now, remembering that moment, she felt a pang of sympathy for the man before her, but in the same second a picture of Danny sitting up in bed, his face white with terror, came into her mind. By chance, Luke had been there tonight, but what if he hadn't?

'Then surely you must see that Danny needs you here! It isn't fair to leave him with strangers at a time like this!'

'Damn you, girl, do you think I don't know that!'

Luke was not looking at her but staring down at the hand that bore his wedding ring. Watching his withdrawn, closed face, the downcast eyes like shutters hiding his thoughts, Jill was struck forcefully by the similarity between Luke now and Danny's expression in the moment he had opened the door to her room on the morning his father had left for London. There was something of the same lost loneliness, the same determination to keep his feelings in check, though that control was much more successfully imposed in Luke than in his son. Jill was forced to admit to herself that, in her determination to help Danny, in her conviction of what was right for the little boy, she had made no allowances for what *Luke* might be feeling.

'I'm sorry,' she managed clumsily. 'I understand——'

'*You understand*!' She jolted sharply upright in her seat as Luke slammed his glass down on the coffee table and stood up, swinging away from her with a violent movement. 'You understand *nothing*, Miss Carpenter, nothing at all!'

He took a long swallow of his drink, staring intently and, she could have sworn, unseeingly out of the window as he did so.

'How has Danny been since I've been away?' he asked, once more the distant, uninvolved employer. 'Have you had any trouble with him?'

'Oh, he's been fine.' To her consternation Jill found her voice sounding unnaturally loud and enthusiastic as she tried to adjust to yet another of those sudden switches of mood. 'No trouble at all until tonight——'

She broke off abruptly as her conscience gave another painful stab, reminding her of the gentle, loving way Luke had handled his son's distress. She had misjudged him badly, and honesty demanded that she admit that fact.

'I think I owe you an apology.' She blurted it out

hastily, wanting the words said before she lost her nerve, though when she heard her own voice she winced at its stiff awkwardness, the huge gap between what she really felt and the way the apology had come across as reluctant and forced, and from the way Luke's eyebrows jerked together in frowning response that was how he heard it too.

'I accused you of not taking Danny's feelings into account,' she rushed on thoughtlessly, trying to inject some sincerity into her tone but only managing to sound more forced than ever. 'But only someone who loved him ...' The words died in her throat as she saw the expression that crossed Luke's face.

'So you do give me credit for loving him at least.' Luke's words were laced with grim irony. 'Thank you.'

'I didn't——' Jill abandoned her half-formed attempt to explain. It seemed that, no matter what she said, he was determined to take it the wrong way—though really, if she faced the truth, she was partly responsible for his reactions. Determinedly she squared her shoulders and tried again. 'I do understand. It must be very hard for you to balance the demands of your job with——'

'God!' Luke's savage curse broke in on her stumbling attempt at reconciliation. 'You've changed your tune!'

'I see things more clearly now—and I sympathise——'

'I don't want your bloody sympathy!' The volcano had erupted well and truly now, and she shrank away from the black fury in his face. 'I don't want anything from you except that you leave me alone! Got that?'

'Perfectly,' Jill said stiffly—and meant it. But her newly-formed resolve flew out of the window when, in a sudden release from the tension that had gripped him, Luke's shoulders slumped tiredly and he rubbed his hand across his eyes in the same weary gesture he had used before.

'Look,' she tried again, not caring if she sparked off another explosion, 'have you eaten? I could——'

The anger she had anticipated didn't come. 'No.' Luke's voice was low as he raised one hand in a dismissive gesture. 'Don't bother.'

'It's no bother, and you should——'

'Don't fuss!' Luke's fragile control snapped abruptly. Then, clearly catching himself up, he added more quietly, 'You don't have to worry about me, that's not what you're paid for.'

'I wasn't thinking of it as part of the job!' Indignation rang in Jill's voice. Something in what she said or her expression seemed to provide him with a mixture of amusement and another emotion, one she found it hard to define, but when he spoke again it was to change the subject completely.

'Tell me about your family,' Luke said unexpectedly.

'There's nothing much to tell really.'

One eyebrow lifted in mocking surprise. 'Oh, come now, you can't mean that. You've plenty to say on things you know far less about.' Jill winced at the sting of his sarcasm. 'Tell me,' he said, and it was like a command, 'have you any brothers or sisters?'

'One sister, Rose. She's married with two little girls—twins.'

Without quite knowing how it had happened, she was launched, the words flowing easily, recounting all the small family incidents, trivial perhaps to an outsider, but important memories to Jill. Luke lounged back in his chair, watching her silently until, in the middle of describing the girls with whom she had shared a flat at college, she became aware of his scrutiny, stopped to consider how naïve and uninteresting she must sound to a man who spent so much of his time in the sophisticated world of the recording industry, and faltered to a halt.

'I'm sorry—I didn't mean to bore you.'

'Did I say I was bored?' Luke reached for his glass

again, regarding her over the top of it. 'So now you're a librarian?'

'An *unemployed* librarian. I've yet to find a job.'

Her already prickly feelings on that matter weren't exactly helped by the fact that she'd done a lot of thinking since she'd come to Stoneroyd. Away from the atmosphere of delight in her success that prevailed at home, she'd had a chance to stop and consider, to wonder if a library job was really what she wanted. It had all seemed so logical when she was at school. The path had led so easily from O-levels to the sixth form college to the library school at Aberystwyth that she had never stopped to question it. Now she was no longer so sure.

'And marriage?'

The unexpected question stunned her, totally disconcerting her. 'What do you mean?' she hedged warily.

'Marriage—you do know the meaning of the word, I presume?' The cynical humour in Luke's voice caught on Jill's nerves. 'I was simply wondering if it had any part in your scheme of things—or do you plan to be solely a career girl? The idea doesn't seem to have any immediate appeal,' he added drily, misreading her frown.

'No.' She shook her head slowly. 'I've only just got my independence—and I'm enjoying it. And I've seen how Rose—my sister—has changed since she married, she never thinks about herself, she's always putting her husband and the children first.'

But that was Rose's way, a small, inner voice reminded her, she'd always been like that. Privately Jill acknowledged that, piqued by Luke's cynicism, she had rushed into speech without thinking. The truth was that she'd never met the man who could make her even consider the idea of marriage—but she'd committed herself now, and unless she wanted to look a complete fool in his eyes she couldn't change tack halfway through.

'No,' she said more firmly. 'It's not for me, not for a long time yet. I like being free too much.'

'But you thought I should marry again.'

The pointed reminder of her own impetuous words stabbed painfully. 'That's different! You're so much older!'

Luke's mouth twisted satirically. 'Nine years, to be exact . . . I don't call thirty so very old.'

His tone brought a rush of colour to Jill's face and she bent her head so that she didn't have to meet the mocking light in those navy blue eyes.

'No, it isn't, but you've done so much more with your life than I have, you've made a fortune——'

'Which you've made only too clear you don't consider in the least important.'

Jill was beginning to feel as if she had her back up against a wall. How had she ever got herself into this interrogation, and where was it all leading?

'I only meant it would be good for Danny if you did marry again!'

'Now you're definitely speaking out of turn!' Luke's voice was a savage snarl.

'But Danny *needs* a mother!'

In the silence that followed her vehement declaration Jill had time to reflect on exactly what she said, to consider how rash she had been, and to nerve herself for the inevitable explosion. Surprisingly it didn't come.

'But you're not volunteering for the job?' The sardonic humour in his question was so unexpected that she raised stunned blue eyes to his face.

'Oh no!' she exclaimed. 'That wouldn't suit me at all!'

Her words brought a cynical smile to Luke's face.

'Don't worry,' he drawled, the mockery in his voice more strongly pronounced than before, 'I wasn't proposing. As you've pointed out, I'm very much older than you and I'm no cradle-snatcher.'

It was time she left, she decided. This conversation

was getting more disturbing with every second that passed, not least because she was having trouble understanding her own reactions. She had denied that mocking suggestion about 'volunteering for the job' emphatically, but even as she did so the thought had crept into her mind that she had been so happy here, coming to love Danny and the big old house more than she would ever have thought possible in the short time she had been at Stoneroyd. Already she was beginning to regret that her job would only last the three months that had originally been agreed and she would have welcomed the chance to stay longer—though not in the way Luke had implied!

But that would mean spending more time in his company, and right now, with her original impression of her employer turned upside down by the night's events, she couldn't even begin to consider how she would feel about that. Much better to think about it in the morning when, with any luck, she would have a much better sense of proportion about everything.

'I'm off to bed,' she announced, praying that her voice revealed nothing of the turmoil of her thoughts. 'I promised Danny we'd have a picnic tomorrow, which means he'll probably come bouncing in bright and early—you were right when you said he wouldn't let me sleep much,' she added with a wry grin, not expecting—and not getting—any smile in response.

'Goodnight, Miss Carpenter,' Luke said formally.

'Oh, couldn't you call me Jill? Everyone else does—and Miss Carpenter sounds so—so middle-aged!'

'Thirty at least,' he murmured sardonically, then unexpectedly he relented. 'All right—goodnight, Jill.'

It was as she smiled her relief, the first natural, relaxed smile she had ever given him, that she sensed the sudden change in the atmosphere. His gaze searched the aquamarine depths of her eyes, holding her attention so that she was unaware of the way he had moved closer, his feet making no sound on the carpeted floor, so that she was unprepared for the moment his hand came out and he stroked the backs of his fingers softly down the line of her cheek.

Light as it was, his touch seemed to burn a trail of fire across the delicate flesh and Jill found herself unable to control her involuntary flinch away from the disturbing caress. The effect on Luke of that one tiny action was dramatic. His hand was snatched away immediately, his dark eyes narrowing ominously.

'Goodnight,' he said curtly, swinging away from her and without waiting for her reaction he turned on his heel and was gone. Automatically Jill tidied up and took herself off to bed, but not to sleep. It was a long time before, worn out with reviewing the evening's events and mentally exhausted by trying to understand Luke's behaviour, particularly that sudden, inexplicable caress, she finally closed her eyes and sank into welcome oblivion.

# CHAPTER SIX

THE picnic Jill had promised Danny was planned to start late in the morning with the two of them packing rugs and food into the car and driving out into the country for the rest of the day. By the time the picnic basket was full the day was very hot indeed, sending Jill up to her room to change out of her jeans and shirt and into something cooler.

Knowing that she and Danny would be alone with no one else to see them, she selected a bright yellow vest-shaped T-shirt and brief white shorts. She had no need to see her reflection in the mirror to know that, dressed this way, she scarcely looked old enough to be Danny's big sister, which was ridiculous when her twenty-first was only a few weeks away. Briefly she wondered what sort of a birthday she would have; totally uneventful probably, no one at Stoneroyd would even be aware of the date.

Danny's impatient voice calling from the bottom of the stairs interrupted her thoughts and she slipped her bare feet into sandals, collected her camera and made her way downstairs.

As she rounded the bend in the staircase Jill was startled to see Luke waiting with Danny, the sight of him so unexpected that she almost missed her footing and stumbled inelegantly. He was lounging against the wall, and the narrow-eyed way he watched her as she descended made her painfully conscious of the amount of flesh exposed by her sleeveless top, the length of bare, slim legs revealed by the brief shorts. Her heart jerked uncomfortably as his cool, appraising gaze travelled over her in a slow, considering way, jolting into a noticeably faster rate until she was sure he must be able to see the way her chest rose and fell with her quickened breathing. As she came to a halt beside him he straightened up slowly, making her once more intensely aware of the height and strength of him, and she wetted her dry lips nervously with her tongue, momentarily deprived of the power of speech, something which she was thankful went unnoticed as Danny burst in excitedly.

'Daddy's coming too, Auntie Jill!'

Jill turned a surprised face to Luke and he nodded.

'As I said, I've decided on a few days off and it's years since I've been on a proper picnic, so I thought I'd like to come along—if you don't mind, of course,' he added with elaborately ironic politeness.

As Jill hesitated, torn between wanting him to come and the uncomfortable suspicion that she would be completely unable to relax if he was around, she saw a wicked glint light up in those deep blue eyes.

'After all those lectures you've given me about Danny, you can't deny me the chance to put things right,' he said lightly, but with a dangerous note under the laughter, one that had her laughing too, but nervously, assuming an ease she was far from feeling.

'Of course you can come. There's more than enough food for three. Danny and I will never eat it all.'

Once in the car, Jill was grateful for Danny's talkativeness. His cheerful chatter hid her own silence and enabled her to concentrate on driving until she had her muddled feelings under control. Her newly-heightened sensitivity to everything about Luke made her supremely conscious of the hard length of his body so close to hers in the confines of the small car, so that she viewed the prospect of the day ahead with a tormenting mixture of delight and sheer blind panic. But as the journey progressed and such remarks as he addressed to her remained casual and even mildly friendly she gradually began to relax and, by the time they reached their destination, had begun to believe that she might actually enjoy herself after all.

As soon as she parked the car near the stream where they planned to have their picnic Danny tumbled out, begging to be let paddle at once. Luke glanced at Jill and grinned, once again bringing about that startling transformation of his face.

'You take Danny and let him paddle, otherwise he'll pester the life out of us,' he said. 'I'll bring the basket.'

Danny needed no second urging. 'Come on, Auntie Jill!' he shouted, starting to run, and as Jill ran with him she felt her tension ease, the last shreds of it disappearing as they pulled off their sandals and waded into the cool water. Soon they were splashing wildly, enjoying the feel of the water after the heat of the sun.

At last, in a brief moment of quiet when Danny had paused to regain his breath after a fit of giggles, a lazy voice remarked, 'Do you two want anything to eat or are you going to stay there all afternoon?'

Startled, because she had completely forgotten Luke's presence, Jill spun round. He had laid the rug under a tree, emptied the picnic basket and arranged the food on the paper plates. Now he was sprawling on the grass, his back against the tree trunk, regarding them with indolent amusement.

At the sight of the food Danny dashed out of the water and scrambled up the bank. Jill followed more slowly, suddenly aware of how she must look with her clothes and hair dishevelled and dripping wet. She could not forget that, because of the heat, she had dispensed with the restriction of a bra, her small breasts barely needed one anyway, and now her damp T-shirt clung revealingly to the soft curves—a fact that had clearly not escaped those keen, observant eyes, making her heart thud painfully as she made her way towards Luke.

'Do you realise you've been playing water babies for

over an hour?' he asked, his words sending her thoughts flying back over her time in the water, wondering if he had been watching all that time, an idea that combined with the way his eyes had been fixed on her only moments before to rock her mental balance, making her glad to hide her burning cheeks behind the towel Luke tossed her, emerging only when she had regained enough equanimity to accept the coffee he had poured with a fairly steady smile.

'Thanks.' She accepted the cup gratefully. 'The food looks good—I'm starving!'

Luke's laugh was warm and soft. He seemed totally relaxed, almost another person, with no hint of the unapproachable, dangerous moods she had come to expect from him. Jill welcomed the change, and yet, as her heart slowed from its frantic race and resumed its normal rate, she was conscious of a twisting pang of regret.

In this mood Luke was a much more comfortable person to be with, but he treated her with the same easy friendliness that he showed to Jenky and probably anyone else who worked for him at Stoneroyd or in London, and she wanted more than that. Hypersensitive to the fact that Luke was all male, and a devastatingly attractive male at that, she desperately wanted him to see her as a woman and not just another member of his staff.

'There are some horses in a field over there,' he was saying. 'One of the mares has a very young foal. I thought we might take Danny to see them when we've eaten.'

'Oh, he'd love that—he's really interested in animals. Another day we could take him to the zoo——'

Too late Jill realised that what she had said implied a future partnership, and expectation that they would do more things together, but luckily Danny chose that moment to spill his orange juice all over himself and in the flurry of mopping up the potentially awkward moment passed without incident.

At last, tired by her exertions in the stream and contentedly full of Jenky's good cooking, she stretched out on the grass and closed her eyes. The sun was warm on her skin, her hair and clothes had dried in its heat and she felt pleasantly drowsy. From somewhere close by she heard Danny's voice and Luke's low-toned replies, but the words were blurred, obscured by a haze of dreamy languorousness that filled her mind. Later, she was never sure if she had actually slept or not, but she was suddenly brought back to full consciousness by the feeling of something brushing her cheek. Her aquamarine eyes flew open and she found herself looking straight up into Luke's much darker ones as he leaned over her from his seat on the ground, one hand resting very close to her head.

'Sorry, I didn't mean to startle you,' he said quietly. 'I thought you were asleep. No, don't move—there's a bee trapped in your hair.'

Obediently Jill lay still while his long fingers gently tried to extricate the insect from the tangled nest of her hair, though really she couldn't have moved if she'd wanted to. From the moment her eyes had locked with Luke's she had been held frozen, transfixed by the sensations of delight his closeness had sent coursing through her. His touch was so light she could hardly feel it, but for a moment the palm of his hand brushed her cheek again with such gentleness that she could almost dream it was a deliberate caress, and her breath caught in her throat in sheer pleasure. Luke almost lay half across her in order to reach the trapped insect, she could feel the pressure of his lean, strong body on her legs and waist, and his face, intent and withdrawn, absorbed in his task was so very close to her own that she felt she had only to raise her head an inch to be able to press her lips against his cheek. The temptation to do just that was almost overwhelming, but she forced herself to lie still, wanting to prolong this moment as long as possible. She felt she wanted to keep Luke close to her for ever.

'I was afraid you might move suddenly and it would sting you,' Luke explained. 'Ah! Got him!'

A few seconds later the bee was free and had flown off into the blue sky, but Jill was oblivious to its departure for in the moment that Luke had turned to her, smiling triumph lighting the darkness of his eyes, it was as if the real world had suddenly faded and there was only herself and this one man in existence. Those blue eyes were so deep and intense she felt she might actually drown in them. She felt crazily unreal, a whirling haze filling her mind so that her head swam. *Kiss me!* she longed to whisper. *Luke, please kiss me!* But her tongue felt thick and clumsy, incapable of forming the words.

But then, almost as if she *had* spoken, Luke's eyes moved to her lips and then away again, and something like a fragile flame flickered deep in their shadows so that her heart turned over inside her at the thought that she might just get her wish. A tiny, imperceptible movement brought his face fractionally closer and she heard the faint sigh of his breath through his parted lips.

'Daddy! I want to see the horses!' Danny's impatient cry shattered the frozen moment, bringing Luke's head round with a jerk and making Jill close her eyes in despair at the destruction of her dream. When she opened them again Luke was on his feet and it was as if that magical moment had never been.

'Get your clothes on then,' he told his son. He glanced down at her where she still lay on the grass. 'Up you get, lazybones—we're off to see the horses!'

Still intoxicated by the sensations she had experienced, and unable to resist the impulse, Jill stretched lazily and held out her hand to him.

'Help me up, then,' she murmured, smiling straight into his eyes.

A brief frown crossed his face, but he bent and took

her hand, pulling her upright. The abrupt movement brought her so close to him that she almost fell against his chest as she swayed slightly, trying to get her balance. Luke's hand moved to her arms to steady her but his touch was controlled, cool and impersonal as his expression and he released her as soon as she was secure on her feet, moving away to catch hold of his son. Once more he seemed to have dismissed her from his thoughts, his attention concentrated on getting the T-shirt and shorts on to the wriggling little body.

Left alone, Jill felt cold as if the sun had suddenly gone behind a cloud, the warm, sensual feeling extinguished by the cold touch of reality. She had been totally unprepared for the strength of her response to those brief moments of contact with Luke, so much so that she had acted without thinking, had actually tried to flirt with him. Now she wondered what on earth had possessed her.

He had made it plain that he was her employer, nothing more. If she had had any doubts on that score then his abrupt withdrawal just now would have swiftly disillusioned her. Any attempt to alter that relationship would not only be unacceptable to Luke, it might also lose her her job, a job that had come to mean much more to her than she would ever have dreamed possible. She would have to tread very carefully in future; one false move and she would be on her way home, away from Stoneroyd, away from Danny, away from—— No! She mustn't even *think* of that!

# CHAPTER SEVEN

'DON'T want to go home!' Danny's small face took on an expression of sulky defiance, his bottom lip quivering in the way it had on that morning when Luke had set out for London. A frown darkened his father's face.

'No arguments, Danny,' Luke said sharply. 'It's time to go. I have to get back, I'm expecting an important phone call.'

'I don't *want* to go,' Danny repeated stubbornly and, busy packing away the picnic things, Jill thought to herself that she knew exactly how he felt.

The day spent with his father must have seemed like heaven to the little boy, starved as he was of Luke's company. For that brief idyll he had had a taste of the happiness and sense of belonging that was every child's right, but now the special time was over. For Jill too the day had been a time of delight, and her steps dragged as reluctantly as Danny's as they made their way towards the car.

She was glad when Luke offered to drive on the return journey, feeling the need for some time in which to adjust to the change that the return to Stoneroyd and the inevitable restoration of the barriers between employer and employee must produce. Like Danny, she would find it hard to let Luke go after the closeness they had shared.

'The sun has got his hat on, hip hip hip hooray!'

Danny had recovered from his sulky mood and was singing loudly and cheerfully on the back seat. Jill smiled to herself at the sound, but then as Luke half turned and glanced briefly at his son, she saw the mixture of emotions on his face.

Risking a glance at Luke's profile now that his eyes were once more intent on the road, she considered the look he had given Danny. What had he been thinking in that moment? She couldn't tell, and that stern profile was every bit as uncommunicative now as it had been on that first journey to Stoneroyd almost a month before. But there had been surprise, amusement—and something uncannily close to pain in his eyes as he had glanced at his son.

*Why* did a man whose working life was so involved with music keep his child cut off from the pleasure it could bring? The songs Jill had heard on the tape had returned to haunt her several times throughout the day, bringing with them a worrying sense of unease when she compared their melodic beauty with the silence that pervaded Stoneroyd and which she was now convinced was somehow connected with the deliberate isolation of the house and Luke's obsession with his own privacy.

A faint frown creased her forehead as she recalled another puzzling incident earlier that afternoon. Luke had spotted a kingfisher perched on a branch overhanging the stream and pointed it out to Danny, the two of them standing still and silent so as not to scare the bird. With its brightly coloured plumage shining in the sunlight the small creature made an attractive picture, but it was the man and the child, so alike and yet so different, that fascinated Jill and had her reaching for her camera.

The click of the shutter was so faint that she could have sworn no one could have heard it, but Luke whirled round immediately, his dark eyes flashing fire.

'What the hell——' he began furiously, but Jill's instincts for self-preservation had been alerted by his swift reaction and before he even framed the question she gestured towards the branch from which the bird had now flown, frightened by Luke's sudden movement.

'It was a kingfisher, wasn't it?' she asked, her voice high and nervous, and noted thankfully the perceptible lessening of tension in his face.

'Yes.' He had no time to say more; Danny had seen the camera.

'Take my picture, Auntie Jill!'

She hesitated, glanced swiftly at Luke, who nodded his permission, but she noticed that he moved well away when she focused the camera again and continued to keep his distance as she took several pictures of Danny then and later when they finally reached the field in which the horses grazed.

She had operated the camera automatically, her mind buzzing with unspoken questions. What incident in Luke's past had made him react so violently to something as slight as the sound of a camera shutter? From one corner of her mind came a memory of the conversation she had had with him on her second day at Stoneroyd, Luke's words suddenly infused with a new intensity. He had been determined that the press should not intrude into Danny's life—so had he once suffered from the over-persistent and unwelcome attentions of reporters and photographers?

It was after five when they finally reached the house, and Luke headed straight for his study to await the expected phone call. Jill took Danny up to the nursery to clean up ready for tea. In the bathroom she caught a glimpse of her own appearance, and gave an exclamation of horror at what she saw. After its wetting and then being allowed to dry in the sun, her hair was a wild, bird's nest tangle, her face had caught the sun, turning an unbecoming shade of pink, and her nose positively glowed. Her clothes too were crumpled and stained, the whole picture not a pleasing prospect at all.

Deciding Danny could have his tea in his pyjamas, she bundled the little boy into the bath to wash off the grime of his day in the country, then turned her attention to her own appearance. A swift shampoo and blow-dry restored her blonde hair to its usual sleek golden cap about her head, then she washed and changed into a fresh cotton blouse and skirt in a delicate shade of yellow. Anything further would have to wait until Danny was in bed, though she doubted if she could do very much about her unflatteringly pink complexion. She didn't relish the thought of dressing for dinner if, as she expected, Luke wanted her to join him for the more formal evening meal, so she was relieved when, a short time later, Jenky arrived with the tea tray, bringing with her Jill's food as usual.

'Mr Garrett said I was to carry on as usual, not to upset Danny's routine,' the housekeeper explained. 'He asked me to tell you he'll join you later.'

Danny had finished his tea and was listening to a story, his heavy eyelids drooping, already half asleep, before the door opened and Luke came into the room. He had changed out of the jeans he had worn on the picnic and was now dressed in a light grey lightweight suit with a darker grey shirt underneath, and as soon as he spoke Jill knew that the change went deeper than outward appearances. His tone was no longer friendly and relaxed but cool and distant, the barriers once more firmly established, and she sensed without having to be told that he was leaving them again.

Danny seemed sensitive to the change in his father too and made no attempt to climb on to Luke's knee or cuddle against him but simply stood silently at the side of Luke's chair, holding tightly to his hand.

'I have to go back to London earlier than I expected,' Luke announced. 'I shall have to leave tonight.'

What happened to the days off? Jill wondered. She

glanced anxiously at Danny to see how he would take this news, expecting tears or sulks, but the little boy was either too tired to protest or so accustomed to his father's brief visits that he knew it was useless to say anything, He simply tightened his hold on Luke's hand as if by doing so he could delay the moment of parting.

'When will you be back?' Jill couldn't quite erase her concern from her voice, and Luke's lips tightened slightly at the sound of it.

'I said I'd be back on the twenty-seventh so you could have the weekend off, and I intend to keep to that, whatever happens.'

His taut expression softened slightly as he drew Danny a little closer, one arm around the boy's shoulders.

'Not so long this time Danny. I'll be back on Friday.' He ruffled the dark hair gently. 'And now I think it's time you were in bed.'

Luke scooped his son up into his arms and carried him from the room. Watching him go, Jill felt a wave of desolation, a sense of being excluded sweep over her, but with an effort she forced it away again. This was what she wanted, wasn't it? She'd wanted Luke to spend more time with Danny, wanted them to grow closer so that ultimately they wouldn't need her—so why was there a stabbing pain in her heart when she saw it actually happen?

Danny must have been exhausted, because she had hardly had time to wash up the tea things before Luke returned. He did not come into the room but lingered in the doorway, his position seeming to emphasise his anxiety to get away, to be on the road to London, as if in his mind he was already halfway there.

'Is there anything you need before I go?' he asked. 'Have you enough money?'

And if there was a question guaranteed to stiffen her

back and put that tartness back in her voice that was it! 'Plenty,' she said tightly. 'I've hardly touched what you gave me.'

Luke nodded his somewhat distant approval. 'I'll be back around five on Friday, so if you're ready by then you can leave as soon as I get here.' A swift glance at the clock had him turning as if to go and she almost cried out at the feeling of loss that tore through her.

'Luke!' She couldn't let him go like this.

Luke turned impatiently, his expression telling her how much he resented being called back. What could she say? What explanation could she give for keeping him with her a few moments longer?

'I—just wanted to say that I enjoyed this afternoon very much and I'm sure Danny did too. He needs time with you so badly.' She saw Luke's face change, his eyes darken with anger, but couldn't stop. 'You should do it more often.'

'It's gratifying to know that I have your approval.' Luke's voice was icy, the bitter cynicism of his words lashing her like winter sleet. 'But I think you should rid yourself of this idea you seem to have that you're here to change my life, make me see the error of my ways. I have no need of a guardian angel to lead me along the path of righteousness—least of all one scarcely out of the schoolroom!'

'I wouldn't be so sure of that!' Jill flashed furiously, hiding the hurt of that cynical 'scarcely out of the schoolroom' behind a pretence of defiance. 'You——'

But she never finished the sentence, because Luke moved suddenly, striding into the room to stand beside her, his face so dark with anger that she shrank away from his approach, turning her head instinctively as if afraid he might actually strike her. Rough fingers caught her under the chin, twisting her face round so that she had no alternative but to meet the icy fury in Luke's dark eyes as she winced under the hard pressure of his grip—and she had thought his hands were gentle!

'Danny likes you,' Luke said dangerously quietly, the very softness of his tone infinitely more menacing than if he had shouted. 'He's very happy with you, so I'm letting you stay because, contrary to your twisted beliefs, I do *want* him to be happy—and if that means having you around then I suppose I have to put up with it. But *Danny* is your concern, no one else.' Jill gasped in pain as his grip on her face tightened bruisingly, his fingers digging into the soft skin of her cheeks. 'You've had all the warnings you're going to get, Miss Busybody—I'm not going to tell you again! Keep out of my life or you'll find yourself back in Burnbridge before you've time to breathe!' Abruptly he released her, and she raised a trembling hand to finger her bruised cheek, not daring to meet Luke's eyes as he continued. 'Might I remind you that Stoneroyd is my home—the one place where I expect some peace——'

'Home!' Jill couldn't stop herself from echoing the word satirically. 'Stoneroyd isn't a home—it's a damn fortress!'

'Maybe it is,' Luke returned harshly, 'but that's the way I like it.'

There was nothing she could say to answer that, and besides, she didn't trust herself to speak. Reaction to Luke's anger had begun to set in, tears of pain and shock burned in her eyes, but she kept her head bent, determined not to let him see them. It was only when she heard the door slam and knew that Luke had gone that she found the strength to move, sinking shakily into a chair, her hands still pressed to her injured face.

Bitter laughter rose in her throat at the memory of her own foolishness earlier. She had thought—had allowed herself to think—that the relaxed, happier mood of the picnic had included her as well as Danny, but she couldn't have been more wrong. Luke's concern, his affection, had been given solely to his son, *she* had no place in his scheme of things. If she had any hopes of things being otherwise this latest confrontation had crushed them once and for all. She had overstepped the invisible boundaries Luke had laid down and he had swiftly and savagely slapped her back into her place. She had called Stoneroyd a fortress, but it wasn't just the house that was locked and barred against the world; Luke's mind and heart were closed against all invasion from outside—and most particularly against her.

And now she knew why it had hurt so much to see Danny and Luke go out of the room without her. She had told herself that all she cared about was Danny, that she wanted him to form a much closer relationship with his father, but when the granting of that wish had brought her nothing but pain she found herself forced up against the hard truth, which was that she didn't just want Luke to find more time for Danny. Foolishly, impossibly, hopelessly, she also wanted him to find a place in his life for *her*.

True to his word, Luke was back at Stoneroyd the following Friday afternoon. The first Jill knew of his arrival was the sight of the Mercedes parked outside the house when she and Danny arrived back after a walk, and when she went into the kitchen Jenky informed her that Luke wanted to see her straight away, in the study.

Luke wasted no time on polite preliminaries like greetings but simply picked up an envelope that lay on his desk and held it out to her.

'Your wages. I thought you'd prefer cash as it's too late to get to a bank.' His tone was remote and businesslike, totally impersonal. 'Take a long weekend, there's no need to be back until late Monday night.'

'Oh, but won't you want me here for Danny's bedtime?'

'I am quite capable of putting my son to bed.' Luke's icy tongue lashed her savagely. 'After all, we shall have to manage without your invaluable assistance for the rest of the weekend.'

'You'll still be here on Monday night?' The question came out unevenly. Luke's sarcasm had stung as it was clearly meant to do.

'Monday night and quite possibly for some days afterwards,' he confirmed shortly. 'I have no plans to go back to London for some time—but I shall have plenty of work to do here.'

'I'll make sure we don't disturb you, then.' Was that stiff, cold little voice really hers? She couldn't help it, Luke's attitude told her plainly that they were right back at Start, as if the afternoon of the picnic had never been.

'I'd appreciate that.' He reached for some papers and picked up a pen. 'You can take the car, of course—enjoy your weekend.'

That abrupt dismissal left Jill in no doubt that there was no point in lingering—and after all, what else had she expected? *Expected* nothing, she told herself on the way to the door, but *hoped*—— Oh yes, she'd secretly hoped for some word, one comment that would make her feel that at least Luke *saw* her. Those deep blue eyes had looked straight through her all the time he had been speaking.

'One thing.' Luke's sudden words brought her swinging round. 'I understand you and Danny eat together now in the evenings.'

'We have tea together in the nursery,' Jill agreed.

'Then perhaps it would be best if you kept to that arrangement while I'm here. It would suit me too, and I can see little point in the two of us being obliged to spend our evenings together.' If he noticed how she flinched at the cruelty of that remark he gave no sign of it but continued imperturbably, 'I'll talk to Jenky about it.'

She was well out of it, Jill told herself firmly as she turned the little Fiat out of the main gates half an hour later. Luke couldn't have made things plainer if he'd tried, and she'd be all kinds of a fool if she let herself dream that things could be otherwise—but knowing that didn't stop her from feeling as if she was being torn in two, leaving part of her heart in the house she had just left. She was looking forward to seeing her parents, and Rose would be there too, with her husband Bill and the twins, so why did she suddenly feel that to leave Stoneroyd was the last thing she wanted?

The answer was shockingly simple. She had been fool enough to come to feel for Luke Garrett more than she had ever felt for any other one person in her whole life, and there was no way that feeling was ever going to be returned. For a moment tears blurred the road in front of her, but resolutely she forced them back and pressed her foot down hard on the accelerator. Rose would be at home, she would be able to talk things over with her— and if ever there was a time when she needed her sister's clear-headed common sense, that time was now.

'Hey, Jill!' A sharp finger poked her in the ribs and she turned, startled, to meet her sister's laughing eyes. 'What are you dreaming about? You haven't heard a word I've said!'

'Sorry, I was thinking—about Danny.'

Well, that was partly true. She *had* been thinking about Danny, he inevitably came into her mind when she thought of Luke, but it was memories of Luke that filled her every waking moment. Her first thought in the morning was always of him, and at this time in the evening, when there was a pause in the almost non-stop conversation, she would glance at the clock and know that by now Danny would be in bed and Luke was probably back in his study, working, alone in the silent house except for the sleeping child, for Jenky would have gone out on her usual Saturday visit.

'Hmm!' Rose gave her sister a shrewd, knowing look, then she reached out and pulled Jill to her feet. 'I've got something to show you. Come on—upstairs!'

She pushed her up the stairs before her and into her bedroom. 'Now wait here!'

Left alone, Jill wandered to the window and stood looking out at the hills opposite, still clearly defined against the horizon in spite of the gathering dusk. Somewhere over there, high up on those hills, was Stoneroyd. Perhaps one of the lights she could see actually came from Luke's study. A longing to be back in the big grey house tore at her heart. Suddenly Stoneroyd seemed so far away, another world, and what made it worse was the knowledge that, even when she *was* there, she was never really part of that world, at least not to Luke.

'You can look now,' Rose's voice said behind her and, dragged from her reverie, Jill turned to find that her sister was holding a dress up against herself, a beautiful full-length dress in a silky material of mint-green with a sleeveless cross-over bodice and full, flowing skirt.

'I didn't want to wrap it in case it got creased. I know it's not actually your birthday until Friday, but I wanted to see your face when I gave it to you.'

'You mean it's for me?'

'Of course it's for you!' laughed Rose. 'Can you see me getting my middle-age spread into this?' Ruefully she patted her rounded stomach. 'It's time you had something nice, you can't go round looking like a penniless student for ever. Well, aren't you going to try it on?'

A few minutes later Jill turned to look in the mirror— and gasped in amazement. The dress was a perfect fit, clinging lightly to her slender waist and falling in soft folds to her feet. The light golden tan she had acquired

from her days in the sun with Danny made her skin
gleam softly in contrast to the pale material and she
looked taller, elegant, a different person altogether.

'Oh, Rose!' she breathed. 'It's wonderful!' Impulsively she spun round, the long skirt swirling, and kissed
her sister, but then her face fell slightly. 'But when will I
ever get a chance to wear it?'

'There'll be a time,' Rose said confidently. 'Why not
take it back to Stoneroyd with you and wear it to impress
this Luke you're so taken with?' She laughed at her
sister's startled gasp. 'Oh, come on, Jill! You're my
sister, after all, I grew up with you. If anyone knows how
your mind works it's me. Do you think I haven't noticed
how your thoughts keep drifting, how you've hesitated
over his name when it comes up in conversation? If
there was nothing behind it we'd have heard a full
description by now, all the details you can think of, as
we've had when you talk about Danny. But you've kept
your Luke to yourself, and I know my sister. That means
he's too special to share just yet. Am I right?'

Watching Jill's face as she nodded silently, Rose
frowned slightly.

'You don't look too happy about it. Tell me about
him—what's he really like?'

'I don't know,' sighed Jill. 'I can't get close to him, I
don't think anyone can. He won't let anyone near him
except Danny, and then only some of the time. He
doesn't seem to need anyone.'

'Not the best person to fall head over heels for,' Rose
remarked wryly. 'What's he look like?'

'He's tall, very fair—just a minute, I've got a photo
somewhere.'

Jill hunted in her handbag for the folder of photo-
graphs she had had developed and had brought with her,
meaning to show the pictures of Danny to her family,
but had forgotten about until that moment.

'This is Danny, and that's Stroneroyd in the background. Danny again with the foals—we went on a picnic and——'

Her voice trailed off as she looked at the next picture and her heart gave a sudden painful lurch. She had caught him perfectly, the harsh lines of his face softened as he watched the kingfisher, the blue eyes slightly narrowed, sunlight glinting on the thick silver-blond hair. Reluctantly she passed the photograph to her sister.

'That's Luke,' she said softly.

She didn't expect Rose's startled exclamation, or the look of concern that crossed her face.

'But, Jill, this is Garrett!'

'Of course it is,' said Jill, confused. 'I told you——'

'No, I mean *the* Garrett. I should have guessed before, it's not such a common name after all, but I never expected he would be the Garrett who'd bought Stroneroyd. I thought he'd be in tax exile somewhere by now.' Rose glanced back at the photograph of Luke. 'This is definitely him. He was all the rage when I was at the Tech, the songwriter of the decade, they called him. He won every sort of award, even an Oscar for a film score. I thought he was gorgeous—that was in the days when he recorded his own songs—but later he changed to the management and recording side.'

And now, at last, it all came back to Jill, the memories that the forbidden tape had evoked buried until now. When she was twelve Rose had had a party for her twentieth birthday and there had been one record that they had played again and again. Jill, tolerated by the older ones as long as she kept quiet, had curled up in a corner, just listening entranced, wishing that the moment could go on for ever. But the party had ended, whoever owned the record had taken it home and slowly she had forgotten the name of the composer of those magical songs—until today.

Suddenly Rose reached out and took her hand.

'Oh, Jillie, don't say this is the man you've lost your heart to!'

'Why?' Jill's voice trembled, the tiny seed of fear planted inside her by Rose's attitude growing with every second.

'He was a real womaniser, a new face every week, and it didn't stop even when he was married. He had a beautiful wife.'

'I know.' The image of the portrait she had seen in Luke's study floated before Jill's eyes.

'But, Jill—he killed her!'

'No!' Jill's eyes were wide blue pools of horror in a deathly white face. She shook her head desperately. 'No!'

'Oh, not with his own hands,' Rose said hastily. 'But he was responsible for her death, everyone knew that. You were too young to take an interest, but it was a terrible scandal at the time. Garrett couldn't keep away from other women, even when his wife was pregnant. Just after the baby was born there was a young singer he'd been working with, she had a child too and she said Garrett was the father. His wife——'

'Marianne,' whispered Jill, her voice just a thin thread of sound.

'Yes, that was her name. Well, she heard about the other child and she disappeared—just got into her car and drove off. They found her body in the river two days later.'

Jill barely registered that Rose had stopped speaking. Could this man her sister had described, this callous, unfeeling adulterer, be the same man as the Garrett she knew, Danny's father, the man she was only just beginning to admit meant more to her than anyone else in her whole life?

'I don't believe it!' she said at last. 'I won't believe it!
It's just not true!'

But didn't Rose's story explain a lot of things—Luke's
reaction when his wife was mentioned, his obsession
with the press, his violent response to the moment she
had taken his photograph? If he had been involved in
such a scandal and the inevitable publicity that followed
he would naturally be very wary of the press afterwards.

'Jillie.' Rose's gentle touch on her hand broke into her
unhappy thoughts. 'Forget him, love, please. You're
asking to be hurt if you don't. He's so much older than
you, for a start, and men like that don't change. It'll be
painful, I know, but not as much as if you let yourself get
any more involved. Don't go back,' she added plead-
ingly. 'Stay here and put Garrett out of your mind for
ever.'

Jill was tempted. She had known she was out of her
depth where Luke Garrett was concerned, had known it
right from the very start, but now she felt as if the water
had actually closed over her head, swamping her in a
tidal wave of despair. She had actually opened her
mouth to agree to Rose's request when at the back of her
mind she heard a young, clear voice calling, 'Come back
soon, Auntie Jill, I'll miss you awfully,' and her head
came up as she squared her shoulders determinedly.

'I have to go back, Rose, I can't abandon Danny like
that. It's only for another few weeks.'

'All right,' Rose said reluctantly. 'It's your decision.
But, Jill, please be very, very careful.'

When Rose had left her, Jill undressed wearily and got
into bed—but not to sleep. She lay awake for hours going
over and over everything her sister had told her. It had to
be true, Rose would never lie to her, and especially not
over something as important as this. Perhaps it would be
better not to go back at all. She could ring Stoneroyd in
the morning, make some excuse, say she'd found

library job, anything. But even as she framed the
thought she knew she could never do it. She had to go
back, had to see Luke again in spite of everything,
because she knew now that she was in love, deeply,
totally in love with Luke Garrett, no matter who or what
he was, and because of that she could endure anything
simply to be with him for the short time that was left to
her.

Rose was right though; for her own safety she would
have to be very, very careful not to let her feelings show.
She would have to be very cool, keep her distance,
which, she reflected miserably, was exactly how Luke
wanted it.

Lying there in the darkness, Jill could not hold back
the tears which crawled down her cheeks and dropped
on to the pillow. If she was honest with herself, Rose had
no need to worry about a thing, for Luke had made it
painfully clear that he had no interest in her as a woman,
none at all.

# CHAPTER EIGHT

IT WAS just after ten the following night when Jill left the Fiat in the garage and walked towards Stoneroyd House. She was still some yards away when the front door opened and the two wolfhounds bounded up to her uttering warning barks that changed to more gentle greetings as they recognised her. Looking towards the house, Jill saw a tall, painfully familiar figure in the doorway, sillhouetted against the light behind him, and her heart contracted sharply, leaving her breathless and dizzy.

Not now! Not so soon, before she had had time to prepare herself. Then she remembered her resolutions of the night before and, gripping the handle of her case tightly, walked towards Luke.

'Good evening, Mr Garrett,' she said, hoping her voice revealed nothing of how just the sight of him had set her heart beating faster, turned her world upside down. 'I hope I'm not too late.'

'Not at all.' Luke stood back to let her past him into the hall. 'I wasn't expecting you yet.'

Jill set her case down on the floor and turned to face him, steeling herself for the impact of those electric blue eyes. 'Has Danny been all right?' she asked.

'Just fine.'

She had forgotten just how deep a blue his eyes were. Was it really only three days she had been away? It seemed an age, a lifetime. She felt as if she had been starved of the sight of Luke, so that just to be with him now was like a banquet all in itself. But she must never, never let him see how good it felt to be back.

'Good. I'd better go on up, then.'

'Would you like coffee or anything to eat? Jenky's out, but——'

'Nothing, thanks. I've had a wonderful weekend and I'm worn out.' Her voice was as light and cheerful as she could have wished, she even managed to switch on a bright, flashing smile. The effect on Luke was quite startling, just for a second he looked thoroughly disconcerted. No, it couldn't be—Luke disconcerted—never! 'Anyway, I'm off to bed. Goodnight!'

Halfway up the stairs, Jill glanced back—and immediately wished she hadn't when she saw the way Luke was watching her, a frown creasing his forehead.

In the safety of her room, she flung her case on to the bed and sank down beside it, her legs feeling suddenly weak underneath her, shaking with reaction. It had been easier than she had anticipated, she felt she had masked her feelings quite successfully, and that bit at the end, implying a full social life over the weekend, had been an inspiration. With luck, Luke would now be imagining that she had spent most of her free time with a boyfriend.

But the next moment her small sense of triumph was swept away by the realisation that she would have to maintain this indifferent façade for another eight weeks. She'd never be able to do it! She wanted to get close to Luke, not keep him at a distance, wanted him to know that she loved him. Perhaps if he *did* know, then—— Oh no, no, *no*! What was she thinking of? If she showed one moment's weakness, let him even suspect she was the tiniest bit attracted to him, then what was to stop him using her feelings as he had used those of his wife and possibly all the other women in his life too? It would be easy for him to while away a little time with her, amusing himself with someone so much younger, secure in the knowledge that in a few weeks she would be gone and he could forget her at once.

No, she had to play out the farce to the bitter end. She had these two months to be near him, see him, and, painful as the time would be, she was not prepared to give it up. Then, when it was over, she would go—and after that? She found she couldn't imagine life without Luke. Time enough to face that when it came.

'An' then we went into this *big* shop and I bought somfing special with an elephant—but it's a secret!' Danny caught himself up hastily in his account of his weekend.

'Well, if it's a secret then you mustn't tell,' Jill said automatically, her mind not on the 'somfing special' but on the rest of Danny's muddled, repetitive report. It seemed that he and Luke had done everything together, never spending a moment apart except when Danny was in bed, and she allowed herself the pleasure of hoping that at least she had sowed the seeds of a change of attitude in Danny's father. If that was true then, in one respect, her time at Stoneroyd would not have been wasted.

The week after her return slid by quietly. Luke remained closeted in his study all day, only emerging briefly just before Danny's bath to spend some time with his son, and slowly Jill began to relax. If all she saw of Luke was those evening meetings with Danny acting as a small, innocent chaperon, then there was little danger of her giving away any of those feelings she so desperately wanted to hide.

But then, on the Thursday night, when the bedtime story had been read and Danny was settled for sleep, she returned to the nursery—and stopped dead in shock at the sight of Luke comfortably ensconced in an armchair, long legs stretched out in front of him and a lighted cigarette in his hand.

'Sit down,' he commanded as she hesitated uncertainly in the doorway. 'You looked tired. Has Danny been keeping you busy?'

'You could say that.' Jill perched tensely on the edge of a chair. 'We've been in the swimming pool all afternoon.' But it wasn't that that had tired her. The shadows under her eyes were the result of long, sleepless nights spent lying awake thinking of one thing, or rather, one man—this man.

'I saw you,' Luke stated briefly. 'You're a good swimmer.'

A rosy pink flush coloured her cheeks at the thought of the tiny white bikini she had worn earlier. She had forgotten that the study overlooked the swimming pool.

'I enjoy it,' she said hastily to cover the loss of composure that the thought of Luke watching her had brought. 'Do you use the pool much?'

He shook his fair head. 'Rarely, I don't get much time.' He drew on his cigarette before continuing with an abrupt change of subject. 'Any luck with the job-hunting yet?'

'None,' she answered dejectedly. If the truth was told, she couldn't raise any enthusiasm for looking for a library job when all she wanted was to be here, at Stoneroyd, with Luke. 'I did send off a couple of applications when I was at home, but I've heard nothing yet.' And those applications had been sent reluctantly in response to the urgings of her parents, to which Rose too had now added her voice.

'Anywhere interesting?'

The conversation was beginning to feel slightly unreal to Jill. She supposed that by now she should be growing accustomed to Luke's disturbing changes of mood, but this sudden show of polite interest was the last thing she had expected. She couldn't relax in Luke's company, the puzzle as to why he was here like this fretting at her mind, keeping her on edge.

'There was one in Devon and another in Nottingham. Bill seemed to think I'd a chance with the Devon one, but I'm not so sure.'

'I should have thought he'd prefer you to get the Nottingham post, it's much nearer,' commented Luke, throwing her completely off balance. Just why should he think that her brother-in-law would prefer to have her working closer to home? Then light dawned with the realisation that she had never told him her sister's husband's name—and now he had assumed that Bill was her boyfriend.

Her lips parted to explain the truth; she wanted Luke to know there was no one else. But even as her mind framed the words the thought of Rose's warnings forced her to reconsider. It was better to let Luke continue in his mistaken belief, much, much safer, no matter how her heart cried out against the pretence.

'Oh no,' she said with an attempt at airy insouciance that stunned her by succeeding perfectly, 'we don't have that sort of relationship. Bill wouldn't want to hold me back or tie me down. It's all very free and easy—no ties, no commitment.'

'Very modern,' murmured Luke, his tone and his expression bringing an ache to Jill's heart with the realisation that she had managed to convince him completely. As she struggled to squash down the pain of loss that thought brought he stunned her by adding, 'This Bill doesn't seem your type at all.'

'Why not?' Her voice escaped her attempt at control and shook revealingly on the words.

'"No commitment",' Luke quoted satirically. 'Now you strike me as very much the commitment sort of person. After all, that's what you've been preaching to me ever since you arrived.'

'In your case it's different!' she flashed defiantly, stung by the mockery in his voice. His mouth curled into that ironic half-smile of his.

'I rather suspected it would be,' was his sardonic response. 'What makes the difference?'

'Danny, of course! A child *needs* commitment,' Jill explained earnestly, leaning towards him in her enthusiasm. 'Just having one means you're committed from the moment it's conceived. There's no other way.'

'No?' A lifted eyebrow questioned her statement, had her biting her lip in consternation, and Luke caught the small sign of unease. 'You can't be that innocent,' he said flatly, the mockery of his first word wiped from his voice. 'Do you really believe that just wanting something to work makes it all come out perfect? So commitment is the answer to everything, is it? You'll have to forgive me if I don't agree.'

'What would you know about it?' demanded Jill, stung into an angry response by his black cynicism, the memory of all that Rose had told her blinding her to the possible consequences of what she was saying. 'You should try it some time!'

For a second she thought the volcano was going to explode right in her face, but then, surprisingly, Luke leaned back in his chair, heavy lids dropping down over burning blue eyes as he lit another cigarette.

'Oh, I have,' he said with bitter flippancy. 'I tried it—but it didn't prove the magic formula for me which makes me rather reluctant to try again.'

Jill felt as if the ground had suddenly been snatched from under her feet. Rose had painted a picture of a man with no thought of anything beyond his own selfish desires, but the bitterness in that 'I tried it' spoke of much more than that. She didn't have time to follow that train of thought through before Luke's next words drove it from her mind.

'Tell me,' he drawled, 'this no commitment arrangement—does that cover physical relationships too?'

Jill's eyes flashed as the full implication of his words sank in. 'That's my business!' she declared vehemently. 'You have no right——'

'No right at all,' Luke agreed affably. 'It's none of my business—but then that never stopped you did it?' The words were softly spoken, but they still had an effect like the lash of a whip all the more so because she could not deny their truth. 'Anyway,' he continued smoothly, the blandness of his tone belied by a glint of cynical triumph in his eyes, 'I'm intrigued. I didn't know librarians were so liberated.'

'My being a librarian has nothing to do with

anything!' Jill snatched at the chance to move the conversation on to less dangerous ground. 'The twinset and pearls image went out years ago, especially for children's librarians, which is what I really want to be.'

'So it seems. I have to admit that it's years since I've been inside a public library, but even so you're not quite my idea of a typical librarian. I find it hard to imagine you working as one.'

'If I ever get the chance,' she countered solemnly. 'I'm beginning to wonder if I'll ever find a job.'

'Are you so desperate to find work?' asked Luke. 'I thought you were enjoying your freedom.'

Once more he had revealed how closely he listened to even the slightest things she said, though she could have wished that he hadn't remembered that particular comment quite so clearly. It had been at best a half-truth when she'd said it, and now, when she wanted to declare that no, she didn't want to start work, she wanted to stay at Stoneroyd with Luke and Danny, it had become something close to a lie.

'It's what I was trained for. I don't want to waste all I've learned.'

'I see. Well, if you're so keen not to let your training go to waste, you could always sort out the library here.' The quiet voice held an unexpected teasing note. 'It's never been properly organised since we moved and I find it practically impossible to track down anything I need. If you could create some sort of order in there I'd be grateful. I might even take you out to dinner as a reward,' he added almost as an afterthought. 'Do you think you could do it.'

In spite of that suggestion of teasing humour he was serious, Jill realised in some surprise. She couldn't see any reason for his request unless he was challenging her to prove herself, and if that was so she was determined to do just that.

'Nothing easier,' she declared, getting to her feet. 'Come on.'

'Now?' He looked at his watch. 'It's almost nine.'

'Oh, it won't take long,' Jill assured him. 'After all, you don't want the books classifying or anything like that.'

A short time later the big, wood-panelled library was in a state of organised chaos with every book off the shelves and lined up in rows on the floor, roughly organised into subjects, while Jill moved quickly along the row, sorting, shifting volumes into order with swift, efficient movements. Secretly she was amazed at the range they covered, though, naturally, the majority were about music, every sort of music from classical to rock and every composer she had ever heard of—and plenty she hadn't. There were hundreds of music manuscript books too, and some of the volumes were very old and, she suspected, very rare.

'You weren't kidding when you said these needed sorting out! I'll just put them in alphabetical order by author—or composer—if that's OK.'

'That'll be fine.' Luke appeared rather bemused by the small, blonde tornado Jill had suddenly become. 'I'll take those,' he added, moving forward to take a heavy armful of books that she had arranged in the required order. 'Where do you want them?'

'Over there.' She indicated the top shelf of a nearby bookshelf. 'And thanks,' she went on gratefully. 'I was wondering how I was going to reach so high.'

From then on they worked as a team, Jill sorting and arranging things on the floor and Luke collecting the books she had finished with and putting them where she directed. She soon found that she was thoroughly enjoying herself, the atmosphere in the room was relaxed and companionable and she had a deeply satisfying sense of achievement that grew as each pile of books was put in order and returned to its appropriate place.

'This is a beautiful room,' she remarked at one point, pausing for a moment to look round her. 'It's a pity you

don't use it more, it's such a waste of all this space.' She
waved her hand in an all-embracing gesture. 'You could
fit a grand piano over there.'

'It was planned as a music room and a workroom.'
Luke's tone was non-committal, his attention apparently on the books in his hands but, remembering the
look he had given Danny in the car on the way back from
the picnic, she felt the impact of his words with a greater
force than if he had spoken more emphatically. His lack
of emotion sent a shiver like the touch of cold water
down her spine, a deep-felt sense of something being
very wrong stilling her hands on the books, holding her
immobile.

'Then why don't you use it as that?' she asked
carefully, her eyes on Luke's strong back, noting the
tautness of the muscles in his powerful shoulders, the
tension in every part of his body.

'I don't write music any more,' he said flatly. He
slammed the books down on the shelf, pushing them
into place with unnecessary violence, then, with a
shockingly swift change of mood turned and gestured to
the pile Jill was working on. 'Do those go here?' he
asked, the dark eyes expressionless, all emotion wiped
from his face.

'That's right.' She decided it was better to follow his
lead. If he didn't want to talk about it she would be
risking his anger if she pursued the subject any further,
and she had been enjoying the new peace between them
too much to risk destroying it now.

But even though she couldn't talk she could still
think, and as her hands worked automatically her mind
buzzed with questions. *Why* didn't Luke write music
any more? It seemed a terrible tragedy that the man who
had written the beautiful songs on the tape should now
concentrate on producing the work of other, and
probably less talented, musicians. Rose had said that
Luke had switched to the production side very soon after
his wife's death, so was that tragedy also connected with

# *Harlequin's*

# Best Ever 'Get Acquainted" Offer

*Look what we'd give to hear from you*

# Look what we've got for you:

. . . A FREE compact manicure set
. . . plus a sampler set of 4 terrific Harlequin Presents® novels, specially selected by our editors.

. . . PLUS a surprise mystery gift that will delight you.

All this just for trying our Reader Service!

With your trial, you'll get SNEAK PREVIEWS to 8 new Harlequin Presents® novels a month—before they're available in stores—with 10% off retail on any books you keep (just $2.24 each)—plus 89¢ postage and handling per shipment.

## Plus There's More!

As a valued reader, we'll be sending you additional free gifts from time to time—as a token of our appreciation.

THERE IS NO CATCH. You're not required to buy a single book, ever. You may cancel Reader Service privileges anytime, if you want. The free gifts are yours anyway. It's a super sweet deal if ever there was one. Try us and see!

# Get 4 FREE full-length Harlequin Presents® novels.

*Plus*
this handy
compact
manicure
set

*Plus*
a surprise
free gift

▼ PLUS LOTS MORE! MAIL THIS CARD TODAY ▼

# Harlequin's Best-Ever "Get Acquainted" Offer

**Yes,** I'll try the Harlequin Reader Service under the terms outlined on the opposite page. Send me 4 free Harlequin Presents® novels, a free compact manicure set and a free mystery gift.

308 CIH U1CE

PLACE STICKER
FOR 6 FREE GIFTS
HERE

NAME _____

ADDRESS _____ APT. _____

CITY _____

PROVINCE _____ POSTAL CODE _____

## Don't forget...

...Return this card today to receive your 4 free books, free compact manicure set and free mystery gift.

...You will receive books before they're available in stores and at a discount off retail prices.

...No obligation. Keep only the books you want, cancel anytime.

If offer card is missing, write to: Harlequin Reader Service,
P.O. Box 609, Fort Erie, Ontario, L2A 5X3

**Business
Reply Mail**

No Postage Stamp
Necessary if Mailed
in Canada

Postage will be paid by

*Harlequin Reader Service®*

P.O. Box 609
Fort Erie, Ontario
L2A 9Z9

Canada Post
Postes Canada
125

the fact that he no longer composed his own music? It
seemed very possible that it was, and that thought kept
Jill silent as the number of books on the floor grew
smaller and smaller until at last there was only one small
bundle to be dealt with in the corner of the room.

She was keen to finish the job properly, but Luke
called a halt.

'They can wait a few minutes, surely,' he said, smiling
at her enthusiasm. 'I could do with a drink. Remember,
I'm not trained for this sort of thing. You're quite a
slavedriver when you get going, aren't you? I don't
know where you get your energy from, you're such a
little thing.'

'Only to someone of your outsized proportions!' she
retorted impishly, getting to her feet. 'And yes, a drink
would be very welcome.'

As Luke left the room she stretched stiffly, surveying
her work with smug satisfaction. He should be able to
find any book he wanted now. Suddenly she was
overwhelmed with a powerful sense of regret that the job
was finished. She and Luke had been so relaxed and easy
together, apart from that one dangerous moment, all the
disagreements of the past forgotten, but now she
supposed she would have to go back to playing a part,
watching every word. Depressed by the thought, she
sighed despondently.

'Tired?' Luke's voice enquired from behind her.
'That's hardly surprising—have you any idea what time
it is?'

'None at all.' She swung round to face him. 'Is it late?'

'You could say it's tomorrow, seeing that it's well
after twelve.'

So it was Friday morning. Friday, August the third,
her twenty-first birthday. A glow of pleasure warmed
her skin at the thought that she was sharing the first
moments of this special day with Luke, even if he was
totally unaware of the fact.

'Here.' He held out one of the glasses he was holding.

'It's white wine,' he explained. 'Not terribly potent—I don't think one glass will have too much of an effect.'

Jill smiled her thanks both for her drink and for the fact that he had remembered that she didn't have a good head for alcohol.

She took a sip of the wine and found it cool and dry and very refreshing.

'I thought you were going to make coffee,' she remarked.

'I was, but when I saw the time I thought the wine would be more appropriate.' Seeing her uncomprehending frown, he smiled and said gently, 'It is your birthday, isn't it?'

'Yes—it is,' she stammered. 'But how did you know?'

The smile widened to devastating effect, making her heart seem to stop and then jolt back into action again at a much faster rate than before so that she hastily lowered the glass she had raised to her lips, afraid she might choke on the wine.

'It was in the letter you wrote applying for the job, remember? So——' Luke lifted his glass in a toast, 'happy birthday, Jill.'

Jill didn't know where to look. To her dismay she felt the colour rushing to her cheeks and tears of delight stung her eyes as she bent her head to hide her face.

'Jill,' Luke said softly and, glancing up, she was stunned to see that he was holding out a small, gift-wrapped box. For a moment she just stared at it in silence, then she raised wide aquamarine eyes to his face.

'I——' she began, but her throat didn't seem to be working properly and she couldn't go on.

'I took Danny to get you a present on Monday, and he wouldn't let me out of the shop until I had something to give you too,' Luke explained. 'Well, aren't you going to take it?'

Awkwardly she put her glass down and took the parcel, mumbling some incoherent words of thanks as she did so. Luke moved away to sprawl in a chair, and she was thankful that his change of position meant that he didn't see how her hands shook and she fumbled with the wrapping paper. A small jeweller's box inside contained a delicate gold bracelet, each of the links made up of a tiny flower.

'Like it?' Luke enquired lazily as she lifted it from the box.

She could only nod dumbly, keeping her head turned away, not trusting herself to speak. He would only have to see her face, hear her voice to know how much the gift meant to her. Fighting to get herself under control, she reached for her drink, swallowed some of it, then finally turned to him, the bracelet still dangling from her fingers.

'It's lovely,' she said. 'Thank you——'

Luke waved aside her thanks. 'Put it on,' he commanded.

She tried, but her fingers were suddenly clumsy on the delicate clasp and she could not fasten it.

'Come here.'

Meekly she knelt on the floor beside him and held out her wrist, her arm resting lightly on his thighs. Coming so close to him she could smell the faint, tangy scent of his aftershave and the soft fair hair brushed against her cheek as he bent his head over the bracelet. This time the clasp was easily fastened, but as he straightened up again he did not release her hand but stayed very still, the long fingers resting lightly on her wrist for a long, seemingly endless moment.

Those strong fingers were so near to her pulse that Jill felt he couldn't fail to be aware of the erratic beat of her heart and the way her quickened breathing sounded unnaturally loud in the silence. What was left of the rational part of her brain screamed at her to move, to break the hypnotic hold of his eyes before it was too late—but it was already too late. She had known from the moment he had touched her that his light hold on her wrist imprisoned her as securely as steel handcuffs, and she was incapable of movement.

As Luke's eyes travelled over every inch of her face she could almost feel his gaze scorch her skin, it was so intense. It was as if the world had faded away and only the two of them existed, and they were no longer employer and employee but only a man and a woman caught in that very special moment of recognition of their difference and their unity.

It was wonderful—and yet terrifying, for she had never experienced anything like it in her life and nothing she had ever known had prepared her for the way she was feeling at this moment. Her lips felt burningly dry and she ran her tongue along them to ease the sensation.

She saw Luke's eyes flick downwards to follow the nervous movement, and in that second knew that he was going to kiss her. Her heart pounded in anticipation, sending the blood pulsing through her veins so that there was a sound like the roar of thunder in her head. She felt his mouth on hers, warm and firm, his tongue tracing the outline of her lips so that she parted them on a sigh, unconsciously allowing him to deepen the embrace. She felt as if she was melting in the heat that burned in her veins, adrift in a warm sea of ecstasy and longing. Her heart was pounding, she was lost as she had known she would be and could do nothing but respond with all the intensity of feelings that had been suppressed for too long.

Unable to stop herself, she pressed closer, needing to feel the strength of Luke's body against hers, totally given up to the delight of no longer having to imagine his kiss, the reality immeasurably more wonderful than her dreams had ever been. Her arms went up to fasten around his neck, her fingers burying themselves in the thick softness of his hair as she shuddered in delirious response to the slow, caressing movement of his hands as they slid down from her face and over her body, burning a trail of fire where they touched, and when Luke slowly lifted his head she remained just as she was, her face turned up to him, her sea-coloured eyes glowing jewel-bright from the flames that had lit up inside her.

Idly he raised a hand to her flushed face, one finger lazily tracing the line of her cheekbone, the shape of her mouth, his eyes dark and unfathomable.

'Whatever would "no commitment" Bill think?' he drawled slowly.

'There is no Bill!' The words left Jill's lips before she had time to think. 'He doesn't exist—at least, not as you imagine him. He's—my brother-in-law.' The explanation came out on a shaky gasp as now, too late, she heard Rose's warning voice in her ear, but shook her head to drive it away.

*It's no good, Rose!* she told her sister silently. *There'll never be any other man for me, only Luke and always Luke.* The words rang in her brain, sounding so loud in her inner ear that she was convinced Luke must hear them too. *I love him, and I want him as a woman wants a man—in every way!* And she knew it was the first time in her life she had experienced such overwhelming desire, beside which the light-hearted affection she had felt for her other boyfriends was like a gentle summer breeze when compared to the raging hurricane of sensation that had swept her off her feet and carried her, spinning and whirling, high in the air.

But her admission of the truth about Bill had quite the opposite effect from the one she had anticipated, as Luke leaned back in his chair, clasping his hands together in front of his mouth and regarding her silently over the top of them, his dark eyes hooded by their heavy lids, hiding their expression from her. He seemed to be waiting for something; waiting for her to speak.

Jill knew what she *wanted* to say, but as the silent seconds lengthened into minutes the words of love caught in a hard knot in her throat so that she knew she would choke on them if she tried to speak. There was a nagging ache of longing deep inside her like some lead weight lodged painfully in the pit of her stomach, and she couldn't wrench her eyes away from Luke's clasped hands. Her gaze locked on to them as if by the force of her mind she could will them to move, to touch her, to give her that intense pleasure those few, brief caresses had taught her only he could give.

'Jill——' Luke spoke at last, his use of her name husky and strangely tentative, questioning, and although the question was one she couldn't bring herself to answer he must have read her response in her eyes, because suddenly he was reaching for her again, pulling her towards him with a force that lifted her from her knees, one foot catching awkwardly in the pile of books that still lay unsorted, sending them flying, tumbling on to the carpet and drawing Luke's eyes from her face to their tumbled disarray. Immediately his expression changed, his face closing against her, and the hands that held her so tightly released her abruptly so that she swayed and almost fell.

'Luke—what is it?' she faltered, but her voice was just a thin thread of sound, not strong enough to penetrate the dark abstraction that had so suddenly enclosed him. Fear clenching her stomach, she followed the direction of his eyes, saw what he had seen, and pain stabbed at her like a white-hot knife.

A photograph album had been flung open by the fall, a single picture escaping its leaves to land at Luke's feet. The photograph was a conventionally posed wedding group, all smiles, elegantly dressed, but the groom was Luke, a younger, happier Luke without that taut, bitter set to his mouth and the harsh lines that now marked his face. Beside him, radiant with happiness and indescribably beautiful in an exquisite white dress, stood Marianne.

'They found her body in the river'. Rose's words exploded in Jill's brain so that she barely heard Luke's savage curse as she concentrated on keeping control of herself and staying quiet, though really she wanted to cry her pain out loud, to wrap her arms around her body to hold herself together because she felt as if she was slowly tearing in two. With an agonising effort she made her mind a careful blank, refusing even to let herself consider what Luke's kiss might have meant because the truth was that it had meant nothing. There had been no love, not even affection in it. It had been sensual, true, but that sensuality had been as cold and hard as the man himself and she would be the worst kind of a fool if she allowed herself to dream or hope because of it.

At long last she had known what she had always wanted. She knew now that Luke was attracted to her as a woman, but the realisation brought only pain with it. The longed-for kiss had left her feeling used. To Luke she was just another conquest, like the ones before Marianne—and the ones after his marriage who had driven this beautiful woman to take her own life. From a long way away she heard Luke's voice.

'As I said,' he declared harshly, the black cynicism in his voice driving the knife in even deeper, 'I tried commitment once.'

# CHAPTER NINE

THE FINE weather broke during the night and Jill woke to the sound of rain pattering against the windowpane. As she pulled back the curtains to survey the wet and misty scene outside, the light caught on the delicate bracelet still fastened around her wrist, bringing the events of the previous evening vividly to mind so that she sighed despondently. For all too brief a time she and Luke had been at ease together. He had treated her like a human being instead of some irritating, interfering nuisance that he could barely bring himself to tolerate, and as a result, acting on the crazy hope that he had finally come to see her as a woman, she had come dangerously close to giving herself away once and for all.

What a fool she had been! She stared gloomily out at the rain-soaked fields. Luke had only to touch her and she had knelt at his feet, her pride forgotten, grateful for any tiny crumb of kindness he might condescend to fling her way. Her cheeks glowed with the memory of his kiss and the feelings that cold-hearted caress had aroused in her, and she shuddered as she recalled the searing pain of the moment she had seen the photograph and felt Luke's total withdrawal.

A flurry of rain spattered the window, making her shiver at the thought of his reaction to the sight of the picture of himself and Marianne. If Rose hadn't told her of his other women, the singer who had had his child, then she might have taken that reaction as the natural response of a man who had loved his wife deeply and lost her tragically. But Rose *had* told her, and because of that she had to view Luke's behaviour in a very different light. For a moment she wished that Rose had never spoken, that she hadn't known, but then, shaking her head firmly, she pushed down such foolish thoughts. Where Luke was concerned, ignorance was *not* bliss, she needed to know the truth—and remember it—so that she could be continually on her guard, against Luke, and against her own feelings.

'Happy birthday, Auntie Jill!' She was allowed no further time to brood as Danny bounced into the room waving an envelope and a parcel.

The brightly-wrapped package contained soap and talcum powder, and when she opened the envelope the mystery of the 'somfing special with an elephant' was solved, for Danny's card was adorned with a bright red elephant, its trunk full of balloons.

There were more cards awaiting her at the breakfast table, for the post had arrived, and a small bundle lay beside her plate. A strong sense of homesickness gripped her as she opened the cards from her family, awakening a longing to be back in Burnbridge with them and away from the tensions that were so rife at Stoneroyd. As she opened the last one—from Rose, to judge by the handwriting on the envelope—a small, folded piece of newspaper fell out and landed by her plate. Puzzled, she picked it up, turning to the card for an explanation.

'Found this wrapped round some old things I was clearing out—funny coincidence, but now perhaps you'll see what I meant. Keep your chin up love. Rose.'

Danny was absorbed in his cereal and Jenky busy watching bacon under the grill, so Jill hastily unfolded the news cutting, knowing with a sinking sensation in the pit of her stomach just what she would find.

'Suicide verdict in Garrett case' was the headline above a blurred but recognisable photograph of Luke, a dark-haired woman by his side. Hastily Jill scanned the report, finding it told her nothing new but simply confirmed most of what Rose had told her—that Marianne's body had been found in the river, that Luke had recently been cited in a paternity suit, and that a verdict of suicide as a result of post-natal depression had been brought in. But it was the last line of the item, heavily underlined by her sister, that told her what Rose had really been trying to say.

'Mr Garrett, who was accompanied by a friend, Lynette Kelly, had no comment to make on the verdict.'

Yes, thought Jill, feeling as if her world was crumbling into dust around her, she knew just what sort of a 'friend' Miss Kelly would have been. She didn't need the exclamation marks Rose had inserted after the word to help her see the truth.

She forced herself to look at the photograph again, studying the woman at Luke's side with eyes that burned with unshed tears. Lynette Kelly was a strikingly attractive brunette, rather similar to Marianne in appearance—obviously Luke was attracted to that type. She was expensively and stylishly dressed, her arm linked possessively through his as she stood very, very close, Luke's silver-gilt head bent towards her dark one. Only a few short weeks after his wife's death Luke had found someone to comfort him—if comfort was what he needed, Jill thought on a red-hot stab of bitterness. She wondered what had happened to the beautiful Miss Kelly afterwards. Had she too been discarded when someone new attracted Luke's attention?

The rain continued throughout the day and by mid-afternoon Danny was beginning to get restless at being cooped up indoors. Nothing seemed to hold his attention for long, and Jill was hard put to it to find something to distract him, until she remembered there had been a delivery of groceries that morning, a month's supplies packed into several large cardboard boxes. A trip to the kitchen secured the empty containers for their use and a short time later they were engaged in a very silly game, with the boxes fastened together to form a 'boat' and Jill, a tea-cosy crammed on her head, squashed into one of them while Danny sat behind her, waving a hastily improvised flag as they sang 'Michael, Row the Boat Ashore' at the tops of their voices.

They were making so much noise that Jill did not hear the nursery door open and so was unaware of Luke's presence until Danny shouted, 'Daddy, get off the sea! You'll get wet!'

Suddenly brought to a painfully embarrassing realisation of just what a spectacle she must make with her face pink with exertion and the ridiculous tea-cosy pulled down round her ears, she glanced up sharply, catching an expression in those navy blue eyes that was naggingly familiar. She had barely time to realise that it was the one that had been on Luke's face at the beginning of the journey home from the picnic when Danny had been singing his heart out in the front seat, before the box in which she sat, which had been straining at the edges for some time, finally gave up and burst, tumbling her out to land, helpless with slightly hysterical laughter, in an ungainly heap at Luke's feet. Calmly he put out a hand to help her up.

'Daddy, Auntie Jill's the bosun and I'm the captain,' Danny announced.

'Of course.' Luke appeared quite unperturbed by the chaos around him, that one moment of inexplicable emotion hidden behind a mask of lazy good humour. 'That would explain the hat. Actually, I came to see if the bosun would like an evening out.'

'Me?' Jill's voice lifted to an embarrassing squeak, causing Luke to raise one eyebrow interrogatively.

'Who else? I'm not proposing to take Danny to a restaurant, and I did promise dinner as a reward for your hard work last night.'

'But——' Jill didn't know how to answer him. She couldn't go, couldn't risk another evening alone with him, no matter how much she wanted to. 'But what about Danny?' she finished lamely.

'Jenky will babysit,' Luke dismissed her objection easily.

Still she hesitated. She could think of no way of refusing, but it was impossible to accept. Suddenly Danny caught hold of Luke's sleeve.

'Can I come with Auntie Jill, Daddy?'

'Not tonight, Danny.' Luke's tone was brusque. 'It's a grown-up party tonight.'

Danny's bottom lip began to quiver. 'I *want* to come!'

'Daniel!' Luke's face had darkened ominously, and quickly Jill bent to put her arms round the little boy.

'We'll have a party tomorrow,' she said cajolingly. 'Just you and me, with cake and——'

'And ice-cream?' asked Danny, half persuaded.

'And ice-cream,' she laughed. 'But you must be a good boy for Jenky tonight.'

'You *are* coming, then?' Luke pounced on her last remark, and Jill's heart sank as she realised that, without quite knowing how, she had committed herself to dinner with Luke after all.

In some small corner of her mind she could almost hear Rose's warning voice, but rebelliously she pushed it away. She had described Luke to her parents as a fair employer, and here was another example of his scrupulous fairness. He had promised her dinner in return for the work she had done in the library and dinner he was providing, so she would accept it on those terms and enjoy it. And besides, she added defiantly to drown out the voice of her own outraged common sense, she *wanted* to go.

It was still raining as she dashed from the cover of the house to where Luke was waiting for her in the car, her haste to get out of the wet resulting in a rather undignified scramble of an entry into the powerful vehicle, but it wasn't that that set her heart pounding unnaturally swiftly so that her blood raced through her veins.

'Hungry?' he enquired as he steered the Mercedes smoothly down the drive, his casually conversational tone in such contrast to the turmoil of her own feelings that it gave her a sense of unreality to hear it.

'Starving!' Her muddled thoughts made her react with exaggerated enthusiasm, and he gave a quick snort of laughter.

'I rather thought you might be. Well, I'm afraid you'll have to hang on a bit, we've a fair drive ahead of us.'

'Why, where are we going?'

'Kenyon House.'

'Where's that? I've never heard of it.' Jill's unease pushed her into unthinking honesty.

'Really?' Luke turned in his seat to consider her, one eyebrow quirking up in surprise. Then his face changed. 'No, I don't suppose you have,' he said quietly.

That lifted eyebrow and something about the way he spoke seemed to catch on a raw nerve.

'You forget,' she retorted sharply, 'I'm only a small town girl, a real country bumpkin! I'm sorry, but that's the way I am.'

'Don't apologise for it,' he returned coolly. 'I can assure you I don't think any the worse of you for that, in fact it makes a very refreshing change.'

'Which was the sort of remark guaranteed to leave her speechless. A refreshing change from what? From all the other women he had ever dated? Her skin prickled with something close to panic at the thought. She didn't want to be considered something different, something that might just tempt Luke's jaded interest.

She studied the man beside her, taking in his appearance fully for the first time. A supple black leather jacket fitted his lean, muscular frame like a glove, accentuating the width of his powerful shoulders and making his thick fair hair gleam silver in contrast to its sombre colour. Under the jacket he wore a white shirt of some silky material and tight-fitting black trousers that stretched disturbingly across his muscular thighs with every movement to control the car. He looked sleek, forceful and very expensive, his clothes a strong contrast to the T-shirts and denim jeans he usually wore around the house.

'Hellfire!' Luke's sudden curse was followed by a swift movement as he braked abruptly. As Jill's eyes had been on him and not on the road she did not see the dog run into their path and so was totally unprepared for the jolting halt which jerked her forward in her seat.

Luke's reaction was immediate. Still keeping one hand on the wheel, he flung the other out in front of her, taking the full force of her forward movement and preventing her from hurting herself on the dashboard. For a moment they stayed like that, Jill frozen, unable to move, then as she sat back in her seat again with a small, gasping sigh, Luke guided the car to the side of the road.

'Are you all right?' he asked, his voice rough with concern.

'Yes, thanks to you.' Her voice shook as she answered him.

'You're very white. Are you sure you weren't hurt?'

Numbly she shook her head. How could she tell him that it was not the jolt that had disturbed her but the feel of his arm, strong as tempered steel, pressed tight against her breasts? He was lighting a cigarette, his hands faintly unsteady as if reaction had set in with him too, but when he spoke his voice was rigidly controlled with a note of cold anger in it.

'It's your own fault, idiot girl. Why the hell didn't you fasten your seat-belt?'

'I didn't think,' she said miserably, slapped straight back into her place by his contemptuous tone.

'Do you ever?' he sighed, running a hand through his hair in exasperation. 'Well, fasten it now, for God's sake.'

He watched silently as she did so, then with a concern that she found positively insulting checked that the belt was secure before he was prepared to drive on.

Kenyon House turned out to be a former minor stately home, sold in order to cover death duties and snapped up by some enterprising businessmen who had turned it into an extremely exclusive restaurant. The minute she saw the imposing building Jill thought regretfully of the green dress Rose had given her and which she had forced herself to leave hanging in the wardrobe, not wanting to give the impression that this evening had any special importance to her. The Indian print skirt, bought at a local market, had been perfect for casual student parties, but it was going to look very out of place here.

Her heart was thudding painfully, her mouth dry with nervousness as they mounted the steps to the entrance hall, but her tension had nothing to do with the elegance of the restaurant before her. It was solely the result of Luke's light touch on her arm in an automatic gesture of politeness to help her up the stairs. Offhand, probably unconscious, it nevertheless set off a reaction like flickers of fire running through her veins so that for a moment the white and gold walls and the soft, deep red carpet blurred before her eyes and she had to pause to take a deep breath to ease the whirling in her head.

'Would you like a drink first?' asked Luke. 'The table won't be ready for a few minutes yet.'

'That would be nice.' Jill knew she sounded subdued and to judge from the swift, slightly quizzical glance he shot her, Luke thought so too, but perhaps he thought it was the effect her surroundings were having on her. After her earlier comment about being only a small town girl, he could be forgiven for thinking that way, and if that was the case she prayed he would go on thinking that, because the idea of him realising her real feelings made her stomach muscles twist into a hard, painful knot.

They were still in the bar when Luke was approached by a distinguished-looking man in an elegant dinner jacket who greeted him with a cordiality that spoke of many previous visits to Kenyon House. And who had accompanied him on those occasions? Jill couldn't help wondering, misery tearing at her so that she completely missed the question the other man addressed to her, only jolting back to the present as Luke supplied the necessary answer, covering her inattention smoothly.

'This is Jill Carpenter. She's a sort of temporary nanny for Danny. Jill, I'd like you to meet Rob Buckingham. He and his partner own Kenyon House.'

Watching Rob Buckingham's face, Jill couldn't detect even the faintest flicker of surprise at the fact that Luke had taken a 'temporary nanny' out to dinner. Perhaps he was too discreet to register any opinion of his guests' behaviour, or possibly he was too accustomed to the different women Luke escorted to be surprised by anything.

'I'm very pleased to meet you,' Rob Buckingham told her courteously. 'I'm sure Luke's pleased to have a new face at Stoneroyd, especially such a pretty one.'

'It's certainly different,' was Luke's murmured response to the smiling glance the other man cast in his direction. 'Would you like another drink, Jill?'

'No, thanks.' Jill shook her head hastily, wishing, not for the first time, that she had a stronger head for alcohol. Even the single sherry she'd drunk was already having an effect, making her hypersensitive to every glance, word or movement from Luke—though she strongly suspected she would have felt this way without anything to drink at all. 'I think I'd like to eat now,' she added praying that nothing of what she was thinking showed in her face. Recalling Luke's quizzically searching glance earlier, she was having very severe doubts about her ability to conceal anything from him.

Their table was carefully chosen to be private and secluded in a small alcove beside a window, making her wonder if Rob Buckingham too knew about Luke's obsession with privacy; certainly they could be seen by very few of the other diners when they were seated.

For the first half of the meal, conversation was kept to an absolute minimum, Luke saying nothing other than what was required of him as her host. He poured wine, making no comment when she refused a second glass, checked she had everything she wanted, but apart from that he stayed silent. It was as if having brought her here and provided the meal, his promise kept, he had no polite conversation to make.

In a way Jill was grateful to him for his silence; she was far too aware of him to find trivial conversation easy. The luxurious room, the beautifully cooked meal, the rest of the diners were all just a blur as all her thoughts and feelings concentrated on the man opposite her.

The light from the candles highlighted the strong lines of Luke's face, deepening the midnight-dark eyes to inscrutable pools in which she could read nothing of his thoughts. As always, she was supremely conscious of his long hands as they moved on the silver cutlery, poured wine or raised his glass. She remembered the gentleness of those hands when they had extricated the bee from her hair, their strength when they had held her face. Instinctively her own hand went to her cheek where the cruel fingers had bruised her skin. Those few brief caresses last night had taught her that Luke's hands could be used in another way too, and the memory brought the colour rushing to her cheeks so that she was thankful for the subdued candlelight which hid her blushes. For one heady moment she allowed herself to dream of what it would feel like to feel his touch on other, more intimate parts of her body, and the sensations that thought aroused made it suddenly painfully difficult for her to breathe.

Hastily she reached for her glass, spilling the wine slightly as she did so and causing Luke to glance at her swiftly.

'Is something wrong?' he asked sharply.

'N-no—nothing at all,' stammered Jill, thoroughly disconcerted by the speed of his reaction. That one swift glance told her more clearly than words could ever do that, for all his apparent indifference, his withdrawn silence, Luke was as intensely aware of her as she was of him, and that knowledge was both exhilarating and terrifying.

Forcing a bright smile, she pushed her plate away with a sigh that surprised her by sounding as contented and relaxed as she could wish.

'That was wonderful! Thank you.'

'My pleasure,' Luke responded smoothly, slipping easily into his role as urbane, affable host as if that moment of awareness had never been. 'Coffee?' At her nod he continued, 'Anything with it? A liqueur, perhaps?'

'No, I couldn't really—I——'

He raised a hand to silence her. 'I told you, you don't have to apologise for yourself.'

Maybe not, she thought wryly, but she'd be willing to bet that the other women he took out didn't get tiddly on one small sherry and a glass of wine—or, if they did, they wouldn't worry about the consequences later. But she was only too well aware of the fact that she had to keep in control and she was not finding it easy, the wine and Luke's company proving a very potent combination indeed.

In the silence that followed his remark she found herself listening more closely to the music playing softly in the background, hardly intruding on the subdued murmur of voices and the clink of glasses and cutlery. She had only been subconsciously aware of it before but now she found the subtle, sensuous rhythms of the tune evoked memories of the cassette she had played at Stoneroyd.

'Is this one of your compositions?' she asked impetuously, not giving herself time to consider if the question was wise. Luke inclined his head in silent acquiescence. 'I thought so! It reminds me so much of——' She stopped abruptly, her cheeks burning.

'Of the tape you played in spite of orders to the contrary,' he finished for her. 'Oh yes,' he went on, seeing her start of shocked surprise, 'I know about that. But then I suppose I asked for it. I should have realised that to forbid you to touch it would only make your insatiable curiosity worse.'

The unexpected good humour in his voice gave her the courage to take a risk. 'Tell me something,' she said impulsively, and Luke turned a resigned face towards her.

'As I said, insatiable,' he murmured satirically. He leaned forward, resting his elbows on the table and regarding her intently over his clasped hands. 'Go ahead,' he told her calmly, 'ask. I don't guarantee I'll answer, but you can try.'

Jill swallowed hard, not knowing what to make of this new, apparently tolerant Luke. She finished the last of her wine and, emboldened by its effect, nerved herself to ask the question that was burning in her mind.

'Why is it that music is such an important—a vital part of your life, but there's never any at Stoneroyd? I mean, you are—were—a musician, a brilliant composer, but there's never a note of music in your home. Why?'

Slowly the heavy lids lifted and Luke's electric blue eyes looked straight into hers as he answered.

'It's quite simple. Music is my job and it's a job in which success brings its own problems—notably lack of privacy,' he added pointedly. 'I discovered a long time ago that the only answer was to keep the two worlds—

London and Stoneroyd—well apart, and the arrangement has worked pretty well until now.'

'Until I came, you mean,' Jill said flatly.

His mouth twisted into that enigmatic half-smile.

'You said that,' he drawled softly, effectively rendering her speechless.

Under the cover of the table, her hands twisted nervously in her fine linen napkin, crushing it hopelessly. Would she never learn to keep her mouth shut? It seemed that every time Luke relaxed in her company she had to ask some question that sent him back behind his wall of silence. Bitterly she cursed the impulse that had led to this retreat—and yet she couldn't wish the question back. There was so much she wanted to know about Luke, the faintest glimmer of an insight into his mind was worth any price she had to pay.

His hands were moving incessantly, straightening a knife, toying with a glass, turning his lighter over and over on the table top. He half-opened a packet of cigarettes, then closed it again with an abrupt movement.

'It was a fair question,' he declared suddenly, bringing her blue-green eyes to his face in a rush of surprise. Luke met her wide-eyed, startled gaze unhesitatingly, his own eyes dark and sombre but with some intense emotion smouldering in their cloudy depths. There was a new and very different tension in the atmosphere, one she could almost scent on the air she breathed like the tang of woodsmoke on the wind.

Luke hesitated, glanced down at his left hand, then suddenly seemed to come to a decision.

'Music used to be my whole life,' he said slowly, his voice husky and strangely hesitant as if the words had had to be forced from him. 'Too much so. It was all I lived for, it occupied every waking minute of every day, and I enjoyed the fame that came with success.'

Seeing her head go back in surprise, he smiled, a grim,

bitter smile without any humour in it.

'Oh yes, there was a time when I actually courted publicity.' The smile faded, leaving only a bleak emptiness in his face. 'But everything has its price, the bill always comes, and when it came I found the cost way too high for what I'd gained.'

Once more those midnight-blue eyes flickered down to his hands, focusing for a moment on the thick gold band that gleamed on his finger, and when he continued his voice was harsh and uneven.

'I was too caught up in my own success to see the demands my fame made on others—and on one person in particular.'

*Marianne.* Luke was talking about his wife. Jill's hands clenched into tight fists in her lap as she fought against the impulse to reach out and touch him. To do so would be to intrude into the private world that now enclosed him, and she felt he would violently repulse any such gesture. He drew in a long, ragged breath and expelled it on a sigh.

'When Danny was born I vowed he'd never be exposed to that sort of publicity. That was why I bought Stoneroyd, why I moved Danny up here. In London I'm far too well known even after six years of so-called retirement, so I keep my work and my family physically separate. It isn't the best possible arrangement—for Danny—but it's the only one I could come up with.'

And one that had come too late to save Marianne, Jill thought, stirring uneasily in her seat, because nothing Luke had said explained or pardoned the terrible way he had treated his wife.

'I know what you're going to say.' He had misinterpreted her reaction, thinking she was about to speak. 'Danny needs more of me—— Hell and damnation!' He pushed his hand violently through the silvery thickness of his hair. 'Do you think I don't know that?'

'Does your business need *you* there all the time?' Jill

asked softly. 'Isn't there someone you could trust to run things for you?'

She wouldn't have been surprised if the question had made him withdraw from her again, destroying the new openness between them, and his sudden silence made her fear he had done just that. Nerving herself, she took the risk of pushing him a little bit further.

'You could work from home, use that wonderful workroom you said the library was supposed to be——' A sudden flash in the blue depths of his eyes told her he knew what her next words were going to be, and his bitter response confirmed as much.

'You're forgetting something, Miss Carpenter. I told you I don't write music any more.'

'But why not?' Jill forced herself to ignore the warning in that stiffly formal 'Miss Carpenter'. 'It's such a terrible waste of a wonderful talent. What reason could you possibly have——'

'I think I've already answered that question,' he cut in harshly, sending her searching back over what he had said.

'I found the cost way too high for what I'd gained.' It all came back to Marianne. Luke drove himself so hard, concentrating all his energies into his job in an effort to block out the past, but was it guilt or sorrow that drove him to act this way?

In the silence that had followed his last remark, he reached for his cigarettes, lighting one and drawing on it deeply before continuing more quietly and in an almost uncanny echo of Jill's own thoughts, 'I used to think of work as my refuge, my salvation, now I find it's like a quicksand, sucking me in. If you're not careful it swallows you whole and spits out the pieces.' He spread his hands in a gesture of resignation. 'That was all Danny got—the bits—what was left of me when my job had taken what it wanted.'

'But just lately——'

'Just lately Danny's seen more of me than ever in his life before.' He nodded slowly. 'You can take the credit for that. You stopped me dead in my tracks, brought me up sharp against what I was doing. That's why I came home that first time. I could have stayed in London— very possibly I *should* have stayed—but I found my priorities had changed. London seemed empty, my work gave me no satisfaction. I found that all I wanted was to be at Stoneroyd.'

*With Danny*, Jill told herself emphatically, the words ringing in her head, drowning out a tiny voice of hope that perhaps he had wanted to see her too. A faintly ironic smile flickered over Luke's face and was gone, like a light flicking on and off.

'So you see, you've got what you wanted—does that make you happy?'

*Happy?* Cautiously Jill tested her feelings. Oh yes, for Danny she was overjoyed, delighted that the little boy now had a chance of the happiness he needed—but for herself? That sense of being excluded was back again, filling her mind, leaving no room for anything other than a stabbing pain at the thought that when she left Danny would have Luke and Luke Danny, while she, who loved them both, would have only her memories.

'What will you do now?' she asked, controlling her voice with an effort because she knew she was dodging his question, and the quick frown that darkened Luke's face told her he knew that too.

'Try to build on what I've started.' Heavy lids dropped suddenly, hiding the darkness of his eyes from her. 'I have to be both a mother and a father to Danny, unless——'

He broke off abruptly and in her mind Jill finished the sentence for him. 'Unless I marry again'—and the pain that brought jolted her into unthinking speech.

'Have you thought of marrying again?'

But that was more than Luke would take. With a

sinking heart she saw his face close against her, his eyes becoming withdrawn and distant.

'I've *thought*,' he said obscurely, effectively putting a full stop to the conversation which was emphasised by the way he pushed back his chair and stood up. 'I think it's time we left. I'll settle the bill while you finish your coffee.'

She watched him as he crossed the room, a tall, erect figure, his silver-gilt head held rather arrogantly high. She noted how women at other tables watched him too, their eyes drawn irresistibly by the aura of power that seemed to emanate from him, then glanced across at where she sat, obviously curious to see what sort of a woman such a magnetically attractive man was escorting. She must be a great disappointment to them, she thought ruefully, contrasting her simple outfit with the elegant, expensive clothes she saw all around her.

It was as Luke reached Rob Buckingham's side that Jill noticed one other person who looked as much out of place in the luxury of Kenyon House as she did herself, a young man dressed in a suit that had obviously seen better days, his tie pulled slightly askew as if its wearer was unaccustomed to such a restriction round his throat. The relief at seeing a familiar face, even one she would not have been particularly pleased to see in other circumstances, was so great that Jill automatically raised her hand and waved to attract his attention. A few seconds later he was crossing the room to her table, a puzzled frown on his face which cleared as he came nearer and recognised her.

'Jill Carpenter! What brings you to a place like this?'

'I'm here with my boss.'

'Oh, very posh! Nice to have a boss who can afford these prices; it's not the sort of place for even a county librarian to frequent, I should have thought.'

Jill frowned slightly, not liking his mocking tone. 'I'm not working as a librarian at the moment.' She felt disinclined to enlighten him further. 'Why are you here?'

'Oh, I'm covering a big do in the ballroom.' His expression revealed his distaste for the event. 'The Lord Mayor's Charity Fund Ball. As junior reporter I get all the best jobs; interviewing society toffs and making sure I tell the plebs exactly how much they're donating this year.'

'You haven't changed much, have you, Tony? You always were the champion of the poor.'

Tony's grin acknowledged the mild sarcasm of Jill's comment. 'And your dad always agreed with me, as I recall. What does he think of his daughter hobnobbing with the county set?'

'I haven't asked him—and having one meal here isn't exactly hobnobbing.'

'Maybe not, but your boss must be pretty well in, it's members only on Saturday.' Tony's tone sharpened suddenly, an almost predatory gleam coming into his eyes. 'Just who is your boss?'

'I am.' Luke's voice broke in on their conversation, and Jill turned to him in some relief. Already she was regretting the impulse that had led her to acknowledge Tony, clearly he hadn't mellowed with time.

'Luke, this is Tony Atkins, we were at school together.'

Luke acknowledged Tony's existence with a slight inclination of his head, ignoring the hand held out to him, which disconcerted the younger man only for a second.

'I didn't know you were a member here, Mr Garrett,' he said, that gleam in his eyes intensifying in a way that worried Jill.

Luke's smile was not friendly. 'But you know my name.' His voice was laced with acid.

'Part of the job,' Tony declared confidently. 'I pride myself on knowing everyone who is, or might be,

newsworthy. There aren't many faces here I can't put a
name to.'

Jill's stomach lurched queasily as she saw the
expression that crossed Luke's face. If looks could kill,
Tony should have shrivelled into a pile of dust where he
stood. Silently she cursed her own stupidity in intro-
ducing Luke to one of that breed of men that he so
obviously loathed.

'You should go far,' he said, and his tone was not
complimentary. Then, clearly considering the conversation at an end, he turned to Jill. 'Time to go,' he told
her curtly.

She barely had time to get to her feet before her arm
was taken in a crushing grip that bruised the skin
beneath her blouse and she was hurried away, leaving
Tony standing watching them, a thoughtful expression
on his face.

# CHAPTER TEN

THE DRIVE back to Stoneroyd passed in complete
silence, and Jill felt a strong sense of disquiet growing
inside her as the powerful car covered the miles easily.
After the brightness and space of Kenyon House, the
dark interior of the car seemed confining and lonely,
Luke's silent presence at her side at once a source of
delight and a threat. He seemed anxious to get back,
driving at a speed that kept her tense in her seat and
allowed no chance to talk. Perhaps he was glad that the
evening was over. He had fulfilled his obligation to her
and now wanted to return her to Stoneroyd as quickly as
possible.

So she was surprised to find that when they reached
the house he showed no inclination to leave her but
followed her upstairs to the nursery where Jenky was
nodding over her knitting and only too pleased to be
released from her babysitting duties and retire to bed. In
the silence that followed her departure Jill felt her
uneasiness grow so that she was unable to think of
anything to break it. Luke seemed abstracted; after one
curt refusal of her offer of coffee he had withdrawn in on
himself, preoccupied with his own private thoughts.

Suddenly unable to keep still, Jill moved to draw the
curtains, shutting out the rain that was still falling
against the window, her action drawing Luke's darkly
watchful eyes towards her. His silent scrutiny only
added to her nervousness and she moved around the
room, straightening a cushion, adjusting a book on the
shelves, tidying things unnecessarily.

'Jill,' he said at last, his tone curiously strained, 'for

God's sake stop that infernal fiddling and come here.'

Obediently she turned towards him, but the look in his eyes stopped her dead in her tracks, poised like a bird watching a cat, waiting for the slightest hint of a pounce before it took flight. A sudden tension seemed to fill the room, holding both of them frozen until, swallowing hard, she forced herself to speak.

'I've had a lovely evening,' she began shakily. 'Thank you.'

'Be quiet,' Luke commanded harshly. 'I don't want your thanks—at least, not that way.'

The blue of his eyes had deepened until it was almost black, the intensity of his gaze holding her transfixed as his hand reached out to grasp her arm and draw her closer until she was resting up against his chest, her cheek on the silk of his shirt, feeling the strong beat of his heart beneath it. For a moment shock held her still, then, in the space of a second, it was followed by a longing to press closer, crush her body up against his and feel his strength surround her, and the despairing realisation that that was the worst thing she could do.

Common sense warred with instinct as his hands moved to her shoulders and his grip tightened. She could feel the warmth of his palms through the thin cotton of her blouse, and even that light touch seemed to burn a searing path across her skin, her throat drying in the heat of the fire that flickered in her veins. This was what she wanted, and yet, because she couldn't trust Luke, it was what she could not let herself have. She swallowed painfully, her mind misted with a whirling red haze. She could not, must not let him kiss her again. If he did there was no way at all that she could prevent herself from responding.

Luke's hand was on her face now, straying over her cheek with a practised gentleness that melted her resistance, leaving her incapable of thought. Involuntarily she closed her eyes, feeling the pressure of his fingers strengthen as, with his hand under her chin, he raised her head towards his. Just as she abandoned all thought of self-preservation the movement stopped abruptly, his sudden stillness communicating itself to her so that her eyes flew open and she saw his quick frown.

'You're trembling,' he said sharply.

'I—I'm cold,' stammered Jill, and it was true, for the rain had brought a distinct chill to the night. Luke hesitated, his grip on her shoulder slackening slightly, and she seized her chance and twisted away. 'I've a shawl in my room—I'll fetch it.'

Not looking at him, for fear of what she might read in his face, she fled from the room. With the protection of a closed door between them, she sank trembling on to the bed, her legs feeling as if they would not support her any more. She felt dazed, physically aching with exhaustion from the conflict of emotions that had assailed her.

It would all be so much easier if her treacherous body didn't keep urging her to give in, live for the moment with no thought of the consequences, but it was those very consequences she *had* to think of. It would be so blissfully easy to let Luke make love to her, but if she ever did she knew she would never be able to live without him, and, inevitably, probably sooner rather than later, she was going to have to do just that.

She had been right not to yield to the longings Luke's touch had aroused in her. What was it he had said when she had tried to thank him? 'Not that way', and she could be under no illusion as to what he did expect in the way of thanks. He had wined and dined her and now he expected payment in kind.

Still sitting on her bed, she reviewed the unexpected turn of the conversation over the dinner table. Luke had opened up to her in a way she had never dreamed might be possible, but although he had answered many of her questions there were still so many others left unresolved. He had spoken of Marianne with regret, but only in so far as his work had obsessed him completely, he had said nothing about the other women and she had seen that newspaper cutting with the photograph of him so close to another woman, his arm around her waist, only days after Marianne had died. She shook her head despairingly. Luke had called his work a refuge—but a refuge from what? From Marianne, from the publicity he so hated, or from the guilt of knowing how he had betrayed his wife? She didn't know, and not knowing meant she could never show her love, because to do so was to risk Luke taking what she offered and shattering it into tiny pieces.

The sound of Luke moving restlessly in the other room reminded her of her present situation and, drawing on her rapidly dwindling reserves of strength, she collected her shawl from the wardrobe and opened the door.

He was standing beside the bookcase, his back to her, studying the row of birthday cards she had placed there that morning. As he reached for Rose's card Jill's heart seemed to stop beating, then jerk back into action at a terrifying rate. She tried to speak, to distract his attention, but she felt as if a cord had fastened round her throat, choking her so that she couldn't make a sound. It was too late anyway; the news cutting she had so thoughtlessly tucked inside the card had fallen, fluttering to the ground at his feet. Luke bent to pick it up, his eyes going automatically to the headline.

From where she stood, Jill could see how his whole body stiffened and his fist clenched over the paper, crushing it viciously before he flung it away from him as if he felt it contaminated him. She wanted to run, anything other than face him, but she must have made some sound that attracted his attention, for he swung round, his eyes blazing anger, fists still clenched at his side. For a terrifying moment she was convinced he was going to hit her and she took an instinctive step backwards, drawing her shawl tightly round her.

'You're quite safe.' Luke's voice was full of a burning contempt, his eyes so dark they were almost black. 'I won't harm you. I have no desire even to touch you. Where did you get that?' he continued in a low, dangerous voice, gesturing towards the discarded paper on the floor.

'Rose, my sister, sent it to me.'

Luke's bitter laugh seemed to splinter the night air. 'Of course, I'd forgotten our Rose—a grave mistake. Just when I thought I'd found someone young enough never to have heard the stories there had to be an older sister who would tell all—and I suppose she did tell you *everything*? Still, what does it matter? It was all in the papers, if you want to find out—which you obviously do—every last detail of who's in Luke Garrett's bed tonight. God! I thought it was all behind me, but it seems even now no one can forget.'

'It—it is true, then?' Jill forced the words out.

'Would you believe me if I said it wasn't?' Luke asked with scathing derision. 'Unfortunately there's no other Luke Garrett that I know of.' Abruptly his mood seemed to change. He ran his hand through his hair and shrugged dismissively. 'Well, so now you know. Perhaps it's better this way.' He turned bleak, cold eyes on Jill's pale face. 'Haven't you anything to say?' he demanded harshly.

'I don't understand you,' she managed, but really she meant that she didn't understand herself. Even now she felt as if she were the aggressor and Luke her victim.

'What is there to understand?' He spat the words out. 'Do you want personal details of every woman I've ever made love to? Do you want to know how I felt when I was in bed with them? Would that give you some kinky sort of thrill? Is that what you're after—to find out how the notorious rake treats his women? Is that why you came with me tonight, to know how it feels—*is it*?' His voice was thick with loathing, but whether directed at Jill or himself she couldn't begin to guess.

'That wasn't the reason at all!' she protested vehemently, her voice cracking distressingly on the last words. 'If that's all you think it was then I wish you'd get out and leave me alone!'

'Oh, I'm going,' he snarled. 'I know you wouldn't want to be left alone with the infamous Luke Garrett. After all, that's why big sister sent you that report in the first place, to warn you just what sort of a man I am. But she needn't have worried, I have no desire to corrupt your virginal innocence by forcing my unwanted attentions on you—though if you're really worried you could always lock your door—I did give you a key, didn't I?'

Lashed by that coldly cynical tongue, goaded beyond endurance by his taunts, Jill lost her precarious grip on her self-control. 'I hate you!' she shouted. 'Get out and leave me alone, damn you! I hate you!'

The words came out all the more forcefully because, just at that moment, she felt them to be true. She hated Luke for not denying the whole story, hated him for confirming, by implication at least, that Rose's version of what had happened was true, but most of all she hated herself because even now, in spite of everything, she couldn't stop loving him.

'Well now, there's a change,' Luke mocked her. 'Not so very long ago I got the impression that my company wasn't exactly repugnant to you. But now I suppose you——'

He didn't complete the sentence, for Jill launched herself at him in a blind fury, her hand raised to wipe the sneering smile from his face. But her fingers never made contact, with an insulting lack of effort he caught her wrist and swung her round, pinning her against the wall.

'None of that!' he warned grimly. 'And keep your voice down, damn you, or you'll wake Danny!'

Impassively he watched her struggle to regain control and when she stood, silent and shaking, he went on in that cold, hard voice, 'I've told you I'm going—but there's something I want to say first. As far as I'm concerned, it would be a great relief to see you pack your bags and leave this house tomorrow, but there's Danny to consider too, and for his sake it's better if you stay until Anne gets back—which means we'll have to meet occasionally. All I ask is that on those occasions—which I assure you I will try to make as rare as possible—you endeavour to disguise your opinion of me and behave in some sort of civilised manner, and I shall do the same. But I warn you that if you put so much as one foot wrong then you'll wish you'd never heard of Stoneroyd—and that's a promise!'

'I already do,' muttered Jill sullenly, knowing she sounded childish but unable to bite the words back.

'Indeed?' She wouldn't have thought it possible that Luke could inject any more contempt into his voice, but he managed it, even on the single word. 'Well, it's good to know that, on one point at least, we're in complete agreement.'

There were several occasions during the next few days on which Jill found herself wishing that Luke had decided not to let her stay after all, and on one or two of them she even considered handing in her notice herself. Anything, she felt, must be better than to live in constant dread of meeting him and seeing the contempt and disgust that was always in his eyes when he looked at her and in his voice when he flung the few necessary remarks he could not avoid her way. Never seeing him again could hardly be worse than this.

Then, halfway through the next week, Luke left for London again and life began to regain a more even balance, her memories of her birthday began to blur a little at the edges and she felt that, if Luke would only stay away until Mrs Logan returned, she could cope with the remaining time at Stoneroyd—and when she left, *then* she would allow herself to think about the future.

It was three weeks after that fateful dinner, on a hot, sultry afternoon, that she and Danny were on their way back to Stoneroyd after a walk, moving slowly because of the oppressive heat, when a car passed them, slowed and stopped some way ahead. Jill watched apprehensively as the driver, a tall, dark man in immaculately tailored clothes, got out and moved towards them. They were still some way from Stoneroyd and the country road was deserted. Danny, however, had no such reservations, with a shriek of delight he sped along the road, arms outstretched. When he reached the man he was gathered up immediately and swung far off the ground.

'Hello, little man,' the stranger laughed. 'Where have you been?'

'For a great big long walk,' Danny boasted. 'I walked for miles and miles!'

'Did you indeed? Well, would you like to ride the rest of the way in my car?' At Danny's delighted assent the man deposited him on the ground and pushed him gently towards the car. 'Off you go then, Auntie Lyne's waiting to see you. You must be Jill Carpenter,' he added, turning to Jill where she hovered uncertainly, unsure, in spite of Danny's rapturous greeting just how far to trust this stranger. 'I'm Paul—Paul Kelly.'

He was perhaps thirty-two or three, with a youthful,

good-looking face, glossy, rather long dark hair and deep brown eyes. Seeing her bewildered expression, he frowned slightly.

'Weren't you expecting us? I'm sure Luke said he'd rung Jenky to say we were coming.'

The obvious familiarity with which he spoke both Luke's and the housekeeper's names reassured Jill and she smiled at him. 'He probably did, but she won't have had a chance to tell us—we've been out nearly all day.'

'Ah, that explains it. Well, come on, the offer of a lift home applies to you too, and if we don't get a move on Luke will think we've got lost.'

Jill felt the colour drain from her cheeks. 'Is Lu—Mr Garrett coming too?'

'Of course.' Paul was consulting his watch. 'He should have been at Stoneroyd for a while by now. He left an hour before us.'

In the car, Danny was already safely established on the back seat, silenced for the moment by a bar of chocolate. It was as Paul Kelly started the engine that Jill received her second shock of the afternoon when he gestured to the dark-haired woman in the front passenger seat beside him.

'This is my wife,' he said. 'Jill, meet Lynette. Lyne love, this is Luke's librarian, Jill Carpenter.'

She should have known, some instinct should have warned her! After all, Paul had given her his full name, but somehow she had never thought of Luke's 'friend' of all those years ago as being a married woman.

Ever since she had seen the newspaper article, Jill had thought that if she ever met Lynette Kelly in the flesh she would hate her on sight. But now, confronted by Lynette, she felt her instinctive hostility melt away before the warm smile and friendly welcome the other girl gave as she twisted round in her seat, leaning over the back of it to talk to her properly.

'I hope you don't mind about the chocolate, Jill,' she said. 'I don't think it will spoil Danny's tea, and I thought it might pacify him—he knows perfectly well that if we're here then Luke will be too, and he was so keen to get home and see his precious daddy I thought he might take the car apart. Do you know,' she went on, hardly pausing for breath, 'I've been dying to see you ever since Luke said Anne had employed you to look after Danny. He was adamant you'd be too young to do the job properly—Luke was, I mean—but he soon changed his mind about that.'

'Lyne darling,' Paul reproved gently, 'you're talking too much.'

'I know!' Lynette gave her husband's knee an affectionate pat and grinned at Jill. 'I always do. You're not at all what I expected.'

Neither are you, Jill thought, taken aback by the obvious deep affection between Lynette and Paul. Just how did that fit in with Luke's 'friendship' with Lynette? It didn't, as far as she could see.

'Really?' she said cautiously. 'What did you expect?'

Paul chuckled. 'A matronly figure, hornrimmed spectacles and sensible shoes!'

'Paul!' Lynette aimed a playful slap at his arm. 'It wasn't like that at all,' she added confidingly to Jill. 'For one thing, Luke did say you were quite a looker, but I did expect someone—well, more severe, shall we say? I have to admit I'm pleasantly surprised.'

'It's your own fault for jumping to conclusions about librarians,' Paul put in as he swung the car in at the gates. 'To tell you the truth, Jill, Luke said very little about you, but when he started deserting us at work and hurrying back up here on the slightest excuse, Milady here was so intrigued that she resorted to fantasising and wouldn't be satisfied until she saw you for herself.'

It was all Jill could do to manage a smile in response,

she was busy mulling over the fact that Luke had actually described her as a 'looker'. She gave no importance to the comment about Luke neglecting his work in order to be at Stoneroyd—she knew, probably better than most, that that was for Danny's benefit alone. But she couldn't help wondering just what else Luke had said about her, particularly in the last three weeks. It did seem as though the Kellys did not share their friend's low opinion of her, so perhaps Luke had not mentioned the conflict between them.

As soon as the car stopped outside the house Danny disappeared like a streak of lightning in search of Luke while Paul and Lynette, who appeared very much at home at Stoneroyd, unloaded their luggage from the car.

'I don't know why you have to bring so many clothes with you,' Paul grumbled good-humouredly as he carried a case up the stone steps to the front door. 'I'd swear you've got half your wardrobe in here!'

'It's your fault!' Lynette protested. 'If you didn't buy me so many clothes I wouldn't find it so difficult to know what to wear.'

Seeing her standing in the dim hallway, tall and stylish in a dark green cotton trouser suit, Jill thought that Lynette had little need to worry about what she wore. Her slender figure and glorious mane of dark hair ensured that she would look superb in anything. Beside her cool elegance, Jill felt hot and dishevelled in her crumpled, grubby jeans and a red T-shirt that stuck to her body in the heat.

'It's much too hot,' sighed Paul, dropping the case to the floor with some relief. 'Close, too—I wouldn't be surprised if there was a storm later.'

Jill could not suppress a faint shudder at his words. Storms still terrified her, she had never been able to rid herself of her childhood fear of them.

'I think I'd better go and see about Danny's tea,' she

said. 'Unless there's anything I can do to help?'

'Oh, don't worry about us,' smiled Lynette. 'We're quite able to fend for ourselves. You go and feed the monster and we'll see you at dinner.'

Jill had turned to go, but Lynette's words brought her swinging round again.

'I don't think so,' she said slowly. 'Danny and I usually——'

'Oh, but you must!' Lynette exclaimed. 'You can't stay on your own all night. I'm sure Luke would want you to have dinner with us.'

Privately, Jill took the liberty of doubting that Luke would want any such thing, but she didn't have the opportunity to say so, for at that moment Luke himself appeared, Danny holding tightly to his hand.

'Now we'll see.' And before Jill could stop her Lynette had hurried to Luke's side. 'Luke, this silly girl seems to think she's not eating with us tonight, and she must be sick to death of her own company and nursery teas. Can't you persuade her to join us?'

Jill felt a strong desire to shrink back against the wall in an attempt to hide from the searching eyes that flickered over her. She was intensely aware of the fact that Luke had seen that photograph too and could be in no doubt about the interpretation she had put on it. But his glance registered nothing beyond a vague recognition of her presence.

'I had thought of asking Jill to eat with us,' he said evenly. 'It will even up the numbers and I'm sure you'd like some female company.' He smiled down at Lynette with obvious affection, the lift to his mouth sending a sensation like burning pins and needles through Jill's veins. 'Then you can't complain that Paul and I only talk business!'

'You see!' Lynette turned to Jill in triumph. 'It's all settled. We'll have a lovely evening. I'm sure you deserve it after all your hard work with Danny. You can't have much of a social life stuck out here, miles from anywhere. I'll bet it's ages since you had a decent night out.'

It was impossible not to remember the one evening out she *had* had recently, and Jill's eyes slid to Luke's face to see how he had taken Lynette's last remark. But he was talking to Paul and apparently hadn't heard.

'I'm hungry,' Danny announced suddenly. 'I want my tea.'

Scarcely pausing in his conversation, Luke lifted his head and nodded a silent command to Jill so that she moved to Danny's side.

'Come on then, tyke. Let's go and see what Jenky's got for you. It was baking day today, so there should be something specially nice.'

It was impossible not to notice how, as soon as she had moved away, Luke turned his attention back to his friends as if she had never existed.

Jill was infinitely grateful that the routine of tea and the subsequent bedtime ritual were so firmly established that she could organise them with only half her mind. The other half was fully occupied. Luke's appearance had shaken her badly, all the more so because it was combined with her first meeting with Lynette Kelly.

Lynette was so totally different from the idea that Jill had had of her that it was almost impossible to equate the two images. She seemed to be no brittle sophisticate but a warm-hearted, friendly woman, clearly devoted to her husband who, to judge from the private smiles and glances that passed between them, felt just as strongly about her. So was the other woman a consummate actress, capable of deceiving her besotted husband, or was she really every bit as nice as she seemed? Instinct inclined Jill to believe the latter view, she hadn't been able to detect anything false in Lynette's behaviour. But she *had* seen that photograph!

It wasn't easy to put Danny to bed that night. The oppressive heat made him fractious; even the good-tempered Jenky seemed unsettled by it as she rushed around preparing an unexpected dinner for four. This, together with the unsettling effect of his father's sudden arrival, made the little boy more difficult than usual, and it was late when, tired and tense, and with a headache hovering around her temples, Jill finally reached her room. All she wanted to do was to go to bed too and hope to sleep through the storm she was now sure was brewing. Everything seemed so still and hushed, the atmosphere close and heavy so that it was an effort to move. Perhaps a bath would help.

She had just dried herself, put on a light cotton housecoat and was preparing to dress when there was a tap at the door.

'I came to see if you were ready,' said Lynette, coming into the room. 'Luke said Danny was being particularly bloody tonight, so I thought I'd see if you needed any help getting him off to sleep.'

Lynette herself was already dressed for the evening in a long filmy dress in a black and gold print. She looked cool and relaxed, unaffected by the heat, and stunningly beautiful. Once more Jill was reminded of the portrait of Marianne she had seen. In a way, she couldn't have blamed Luke if he *had* turned to this woman who was so like the beautiful wife he had lost.

'What are you going to wear? I hope you don't mind my asking, but I'm fascinated by other people's clothes—I was a model before I married Paul. Can I look?' And before Jill could stop her she had opened the wardrobe door and was browsing through its contents.

'Oh yes!' Lynette almost pounced on the green dress. 'This is perfect!'

'Well, I had thought——' Jill indicated the Indian

print skirt which she had resigned herself to wearing yet again.

'No,' the other girl said firmly. 'The green one.'

Removing it from the wardrobe, she laid it carefully across the bed, giving Jill a concerned look as she straightened up. 'You look worn out, poor thing. You really need a night off. Look, why don't I do your hair and make-up for you?'

'Oh no,' Jill coloured faintly, 'don't bother.'

'No bother,' Lynette assured her. 'And I *do* know what I'm doing.' She put a cushion on the seat of a chair and patted it. 'You just sit here and relax while I get to work. It'll give you a chance to get your feet up for a minute.

'We always have a proper dressed up dinner when we're at Stoneroyd,' Lynette chattered blithely as Jill submitted to her ministrations. 'It was a custom I started, otherwise Luke would simply have spent the whole night in his study, working, and more often than not Paul would join him—you have beautiful skin, you know, and I'd *kill* for your bones—Luke didn't like the idea too much at first, I suppose just the three of us being there like that brought home to him that Marianne wasn't there any more. But I had to do something to stop him burying himself in his work so much. Don't move——' she added as Jill shifted involuntarily in her seat. 'I've nearly finished, and there's no rush, Luke and Paul will wait.'

Jill subsided again, but this time she no longer felt the relaxing effect of Lynette's gentle hands. The mention of Marianne had revived memories she didn't want to recall. Her stomach, already taut with tension, twisted itself into even tighter knots as she thought of that damning newspaper photograph—and yet Lynette had implied that Luke had mourned his wife deeply, which forced Jill to reconsider everything Luke had said on the night he had taken her out to dinner. Oh, Rose, could you have got it all wrong? She directed her thoughts towards her sister, knowing there was no hope of an answer.

'There now!' Lynette stood back to admire her handiwork. 'Put on your dress and then I'll do your hair—you don't mind my being here, do you?' she added, misreading Jill's hesitation as she picked up the green dress.

'Oh no,' Jill hastened to reassure her, and the truth was that she didn't mind. She had shared a bedroom in her college flat and neither she nor Daisy had ever thought twice about dressing or undressing in front of each other. But they had been friends for years and she had known Lynette for barely a few hours but—here was the strange thing—she felt as if she had known her so much longer, was as at ease with her as she had always been with Daisy, which made it still harder to imagine her as an unfaithful wife who had indulged in an affair with her husband's best friend.

'Hair now,' Lynette broke in on her thoughts. 'I'm enjoying this. It's like having a sister again.'

Jill had nodded smilingly, remembering other shared 'titivating' sessions with Rose, before something about Lynette's turn of phrase struck her as slightly odd. But the hairdryer had been switched on, its noise destroying any possible chance to talk, before she could work out just what it was that had left her with a large question mark in her mind.

'There you are!' Lynette swung Jill in the direction of the mirror and the younger girl found herself staring at a reflection that seemed like that of another person. She was not quite sure what magic Lynette had used, but, whatever it was, it had worked miracles. Her skin looked smooth and golden, her eyes enormous, the subtle blend of dark and light green eyeshadows toning exactly with her dress. Her lashes seemed twice as long under their coating of mascara and her cheeks and mouth were tinted a soft, delicate pink. The healthy, tomboyish student had vanished completely, and in her place was a stunningly sensual and totally feminine woman.

'Just one thing,' added Lynette. 'You need a bracelet or something—you have such small wrists, you should emphasise them.'

For a second Jill thought of saying no, then, reluctantly, she fetched the gold bracelet Luke had given her from its box in the drawer where she had left it ever since her birthday.

'What a lovely thing! It's just perfect,' Lynette exclaimed when the delicate bracelet was round Jill's wrist. She turned briefly to check her own appearance in the mirror. 'Come on, let's go and see if they think we're worth waiting for!'

Luke was pouring a drink for Paul when Jill followed Lynette into the garden room, but he paused, the decanter still half raised as she hesitated in the doorway, his eyes going straight to her face in a searching, narrow-eyed scrutiny that set her whole body tingling with reaction. For a few seconds that intent scrutiny was concentrated on her face, but then Luke's eyes moved, travelling slowly over the rest of her body in a long, considering survey. For a glorious moment Jill was overwhelmed by a euphoric sensation of power at the realisation that she had at last got through to him; had, for this short time at least, made him see her as a woman. The knowledge brought with it such an intoxicating sensation of happiness that she flashed a dazzling smile straight into his eyes, an act which clearly disconcerted him even more, bringing a frown to his face.

And that frown, slight as it was, crushed Jill's rising spirits, his own cynical admission of the popular interest in the women who had shared his bed turning her triumph suddenly sour. She didn't want him to think of her in that way and was overwhelmed with a longing to tear off the beautiful dress and return to the safety of her usual inconspicious appearance. But it was too late. Paul had already moved forward to take her hand and draw her into the room.

'You look lovely,' he told her sincerely. 'Don't you agree, Luke?'

'Oh, yes.' Luke's eyes had never left Jill's face, she was sure he had read her cowardly impulse to run in her eyes. 'Quite a transformation, the duckling into the swan,' he said coolly.

Marianne had been a swan, a beautiful, elegant creature, and look what had happened to her, Jill thought on a wave of rising panic.

'Now I'll not allow that!' protested Lynette laughingly. 'We all know it was an *ugly* duckling who changed into a swan. You're never trying to imply that anyone could describe Jill that way?'

Luke shrugged slightly. 'I have to admit that when I first saw her, from the back I admit, I might have thought she was a boy if it hadn't been for the outrageous colour of her jeans—but I've had to rethink my ideas since then, about a lot of things—— Sherry, Jill?'

Jill could only nod, her mind too numbed by the swift succession of moods, from sensual admiration, to his mocking comments on her appearance, and finally to bland social politeness, leaving that final cryptic comment hanging in the air, to be able to form any words to answer him. As Luke handed her the glass their fingers touched briefly and she could not restrain her involuntary recoil from him, the slight contact making her feel as if she had brushed her hand against an exposed live electric wire, and she drew back as if she had been burned, making Luke's lips curl cynically as he noticed the slight movement.

'I must ask you, Jill,' Lynette's voice shattered the almost tangible tension, 'where did you get that bracelet—I think it's quite beautiful.'

Jill's eyes went to Luke's face, but his eyes were hooded, unreadable. 'Mr—Luke gave it to me.'

'Did he!' Lynette turned to Luke, a questioning gleam in her eyes.

'I gave Jenky a present for her birthday too,' Luke stated quietly, 'so you can forget any matchmaking schemes you might be hatching.'

'Would I do any such thing?' teased Lynette, her expression innocent.

'I wouldn't put it past you.' Luke's dark blue eyes smiled down into Lynette's brown ones in a way that tugged at Jill's heart.

There *was* something between these two, but she doubted if it was the sordid, ambiguously named 'friendship' of the newspaper report. If Lynette had ever been Luke's mistress, now discarded, then surely they would not be so close now, and Paul did not seem the sort of man who could bring his wife to the home of her ex-lover, particularly not when that man was also his friend.

Surreptitiously Jill considered Luke as he continued his conversation with Lynette. He was leaning back in his chair, very much at his ease, dressed as usual in dark colours, the black of his suit and shirt contrasting sharply with the rather bright red and white striped shirt Paul wore. With a jolt of memory she realised that Paul and Lynette must have been included in the 'arty types' who had so intrigued Mrs Dawson, and she smiled privately at the thought.

'And what are you grinning at?' Paul broke in on her thoughts.

'Oh, just a comment someone I know made about visitors to Stoneroyd. I've just realised she must have meant you and Lynette.'

She was reluctant to say any more, but Paul pressed her to do so, laughing aloud in delight at being described as an 'arty type'.

'She'd be bitterly disappointed to know that I'm not 'arty' at all. I stick to the technical side of things and leave the artistic field to Luke, that's his area, after all. Tell me,' he added, obviously curious, 'what else does local gossip say about us—Luke, for instance?'

Flattered by his interest, Jill found herself relaxing and gave him a vivid sketch of Mary Dawson's vain attempts to find out more about Luke, dropping into the local accent when she used the postmistress's actual words to describe him and her dire warnings that 'them up at Stoneroyd must have summat to hide, else they'd not bury themselves away up there like that.'

'And what do *you* think I have to hide?' a quiet voice put into the conversation, and to Jill's intense embarrassment she found that Luke had been listening to every word she had said.

'I've no idea—nothing,' she said nervously, bright patches of colour burning high up on her cheeks. But Luke did not seem angry, rather, he appeared mildly amused.

'Bodies in the cellar, perhaps?' he suggested, a glint of wicked humour lightening the darkness of his eyes. 'Or a few orgies when there's a full moon? She's not going to believe you when you tell her we're really quite normal.'

Was that some sort of test? Did he still suspect she would betray his privacy in some way? 'I won't be telling her anything!' Jill retorted indignantly. 'I don't join in the local scandalmongering.'

'I'm glad to hear it,' commented Luke drily, his expression perhaps a little more friendly than before or, rather, a shade less hostile.

'This Mrs Dawson's going to have a field day when all

the equipment arrives,' Paul put in. 'Then she's really going to wonder what sort of arty goings on Luke's up to!'

'Equipment?' Jill glanced questioningly at Luke and caught the swift reproving frown he shot in his friend's direction, a frown that Lynette missed.

'Yes, the musical equipment. Piano, keyboards, synthesiser, and of course Luke's old guitar. We're going to fit the workroom out properly at last.'

'But why——' Jill's sea-coloured eyes were clouded with confusion. Why was Luke doing this after all this time?

But at that moment the gong sounded in the hall, and Luke stood up immediately as if he was grateful for the chance to break off the conversation.

'It seems dinner is ready,' he said. 'Shall we go in?'

# CHAPTER ELEVEN

THROUGHOUT the meal Jill found that her company was monopolised by Paul Kelly. He was a pleasant companion, one who was clearly interested in her as a person and who asked intelligent questions about her training course as a librarian.

'It's a pity you're dead set on being a children's librarian,' he said at one point, making Jill realise that in her attempt to cover up her own uncertainty about whether she really wanted any such job she had put across an enthusiasm she was in fact very far from feeling. 'We could really use someone to organise all the manuscripts we have to deal with—and Luke will need someone to keep things in order up here when he moves the bulk of his work to Stoneroyd.'

There it was again, a reference to the mysterious changes that were about to take place and about which she knew nothing at all. Not knowing what Paul was talking about, Jill reacted quickly to his other suggestion.

'Well, don't put my name forward! I'd hate Luke to think I was angling for a job.'

'I don't see why that should worry you. Luke was pretty impressed by the way you handled the library here, ready for——'

Ready for what? Not being sure and not really certain she wanted to know, Jill rushed on hastily, 'That was nothing, just a tidying-up operation, you couldn't call it librarianship. And anyway,' her voice cracked distressingly, 'I don't think Luke would want me working for him in London.'

'Why ever not?'

'Well——' Jill looked down at her plate, pushing her food around it uneasily, 'we don't exactly get on.' And if ever there was an understatement, she thought miserably, then that was it. 'I don't think he even likes me.'

A sudden sound that might have been a laugh or an exclamation or a mixture of the two brought her bewildered eyes to Paul's face in time to see the swift glance he shot in the direction of Luke, deep in conversation with Lynette and oblivious to the other two at the table.

'That's not the impression I got,' he said softly. 'But I can see that things might come across differently to you. Luke's not a man who finds it easy to show his feelings, and this is the first time there's been another woman in his life since Marianne. It's only natural if it revives a few painful memories.'

'But I thought Luke and his wife——!' It was Jill's turn to glance nervously in Luke's direction, thankful to see that he remained absorbed in what Lynette was saying. 'I thought he didn't care too much for Marianne,' she blurted out without thinking. 'There were all those other women——' The words died on her lips at Paul's sigh.

'Those old stories again! Jill love, you shouldn't believe everything you read in the papers. Luke was devoted to Marianne, he adored her, and he was never unfaithful to her. There were plenty of women before Marianne, plenty of stories for the papers, and I'm afraid mud sticks. He could never live down his reputation even when he was married.'

'But that singer—the one who had his child?'

'That was never his child!' Anger rang in Paul's voice for all he hadn't raised it above a quiet conversational level. 'She and Luke had a brief affair before he met Marianne and she wanted him back. Blood tests soon

proved the baby wasn't Luke's, but of course the papers
weren't interested in printing that.'

'Then why did Marianne kill herself?' Jill's voice was
just a whisper.

'Because she was a very unhappy woman—but not
because of Luke. I know Luke blames himself, he
believes his fame came between them, and in a way it's
true. Marianne was jealous of his success. She couldn't
handle the publicity either. She believed all the stories in
the papers because she wanted to, she enjoyed the image
of herself as the wronged wife and she made Luke's life
hell; he could never do anything right. She'd always had
attacks of depression, even as a child she had terrible
black moods, and it was a struggle to get her out of them.
When Danny was conceived she hated being pregnant,
she rejected him from the moment he was born, and of
course post-natal depression only made things worse. In
the end I don't think she really knew what she was
doing.'

Jill reached for her wine glass and drank from it
hastily. She felt as if the room was spinning round her. If
only it was true; she desperately *wanted* it to be true—
but even if it was it wouldn't help her now. She had
thought Luke was incapable of love and had reacted
with fear, denying what she really felt. She had rejected
Luke violently, and he was not the sort of man to take
that rejection easily. He was not likely to put his head on
the block a second time.

'Why should I believe you?' she asked shakily, and
saw Paul's eyes widen in surprise.

'I thought you knew,' he said. 'I knew Marianne
better than most. After all, I married her sister.'

Jill's eyes were just wide sea-pools of shock in an ashen
face and as she glanced across at Lynette again she took
an unwise gulp at her wine to steady her nerves. Now
that she knew, it seemed impossible that she had never

uessed. When she had first seen the newspaper photograph of Lynette, it had made her think of Marianne, but she had simply assumed that both women were the type that attracted Luke. Now, when it was too late, she could see the similarity was stronger than that, it was there in the hair, the eyes, the shape of the face. What a different interpretation she had to put on that photograph now—not two lovers heedless of public opinion but two people, already part of the same family, drawn together by a tragedy that had struck at them both.

'Oh God!' she whispered to herself, thinking back to the night Luke had taken her out to dinner, the night he had discovered the news cutting. How much different might things have been if she had known then that Lynette was Marianne's sister? But she hadn't known and, like everyone else, by believing the half-truths printed in the paper had driven Luke away from her once and for all. Hot tears stung her eyes and she bent her head to hide them.

'Hey, I didn't mean to upset you!' Paul sounded concerned. 'What is it?' But when Jill could only shake her head dumbly, too distraught to speak, he added gently, 'Whatever it is, it isn't the end of the world. Have some more wine and forget about it.'

But as he raised the bottle to pour the wine a long-fingered hand was placed firmly over the top of Jill's glass.

'She's had enough,' Luke stated quietly.

A white-hot knife stabbed deep in Jill's heart. Only a few seconds before she'd allowed herself to dream that if Luke had never found the news cutting things might have been different; now she was brought up hard against reality. It could never have been any other way; never have been how she had dreamed. Luke had barely acknowledged her presence at the table until now, when

with one small comment he had condescendingly
reduced her status in Paul's eyes, making her feel very
young and very foolish. Her private admission that he
was right, that she *had* had as much to drink as she could
handle, did nothing to control the fierce flame of anger
at Luke's arrogant gesture that burned away the hurt.
She wasn't going to be dictated to in this way!

Rebelliously she pulled her glass from under his
restraining hand and held it out to Paul, glaring
defiantly at Luke as she did so. For a second their eyes
locked and she felt a shiver of alarm at what she saw
there, the glow of the candles suddenly dimmed before
the flame of cold fury that blazed in the midnight-blue
depths. For a long, taut moment Luke's hand remained
suspended as if still covering the glass, the few drops of
wine that had splashed on to it glistening like blood
against his skin, then at last he moved, turning away
from her to pick up a napkin and carefully wipe the
liquid from his fingers. The implication of his action was
only too clear; he was totally dissociating himself from
her.

'I *would* like some more wine, please,' Jill said firmly,
exerting every ounce of control she possessed to ensure
that her voice remained steady and clear.

When her glass was full she raised it to her lips,
praying that no one would see the way her hand shook,
and took a long drink, then almost immediately wished
she hadn't. The room seemed to tilt and blur and she
closed her eyes swiftly against the sensation, only to
open them at once when she found that made matters
much worse. Hastily she shot a surreptitious glance at
Luke, terrified that he might have seen her reaction, but
he remained turned away from her, his attention
apparently concentrated once more on Lynette. Carefully Jill set her glass down, but her control was not as
complete as she had thought and it crashed against her

plate, the noise drawing Luke's eyes to her swiftly, a dark frown creasing the space between his brows.

She tried to meet his dark eyes with a look that was both challenging and triumphant, but her smile faded swiftly before the icy contempt that was so clearly stamped on his face. Nervously she dropped her gaze to her plate, picking up her spoon and pushing the food aimlessly round on it.

'It doesn't suit you,' Luke said softly, so softly that neither Lynette nor Paul could hear him.

'What doesn't?' Jill muttered sullenly, deliberately not looking at him.

'This sophisticated woman of the world act.' The dangerous note in his voice should have warned her, but she was past caring what he thought and her head came up sharply.

'It isn't an act!'

He raised a surprised and sardonically questioning eyebrow and smiled, and she didn't like the smile, not one little bit.

'I see,' he said drily. 'Forgive me, but I had a rather different impression. In that case,' he went on, his voice a deceptively silky drawl, 'I hope the wine is to your taste. There's a very good brandy to go with the coffee too, you should enjoy that.'

Mentally Jill quailed at the thought, but she had no intention of letting him see how she was feeling.

'I'm sure I will,' she said archly, flashing him her brightest smile.

Picking up her wine glass once more, she raised it lightly and waved it almost under his nose.

'Cheers!' she said gaily.

For a moment she thought she had gone too far. The blue eyes narrowed until they were nothing but slits in a face that was white with suppressed anger, and when

Luke moved she shrank back in her chair as if afraid he might strike her.

But he only pushed back his chair with a savage movement and stood up, thrusting his clenched fists into the pockets of his jacket as if he didn't trust himself not to use them. When he finally spoke his tone was smooth, the controlled violence there had been in him only seconds before completely ironed out of it.

'We'll have coffee in the garden room,' he said, once more the perfect host. 'If everyone's ready we'll go in.'

As the others left the room Jill lingered at the table, not too sure whether her legs, which now had a distinctly cotton-woolish feeling about them, would support her if she stood up. She couldn't bear the thought of showing Luke he had been right when he'd said she'd had enough to drink—and he *had* been right, damn him!

She looked down at her glass, still half full of wine, and the thought of swallowing any more of the rich red liquid nauseated her. Carefully, testing her legs, she got up and emptied the wine into a convenient plant pot before making her way to the garden room, the empty glass dangling nonchalantly from fingers that were not quite as steady as she could have wished.

The glass patio doors on to the terrace were wide open in a vain attempt to let some air into the room and reduce the oppressive heat. Although it was now almost ten, there had been no lessening of the sultry atmosphere which seemed to have grown heavier as the day progressed. Remembering how Paul had predicted a storm, Jill shuddered; thunder was something she couldn't cope with on top of everything else.

Luke was leaning across the back of one of the chairs to light Paul's cigarette, but he straightened up as Jill came in, his eyes going to the empty wine glass in her hand, his expression darkening perceptibly. Let him

hink what he liked! Jill told herself. She didn't care! But
ll the same she felt a quiver of apprehension as she saw
he way the muscles in his jaw tightened.

As she placed her glass on the sideboard she noticed
another one, containing a generous measure of brandy,
standing on a tray. As the others already had glasses in
their hands she could only assume that the brandy was
meant for her and, knowing that she really couldn't face
t, she decided that her best policy was simply to ignore it
and turned away.

'No brandy, Jill?' Luke's voice was cool, his dark,
watchful eyes missing nothing of her reaction. The
satirically taunting tone lit the spark of anger inside her
once more, making her forget her wiser resolution.

'Oh, is this mine?' she asked blithely. 'Thanks.'
Holding the glass gingerly as if afraid it might explode in
her face, she moved to sit opposite Lynette.

'This is the life,' sighed Paul contentedly, leaning
back in his chair and stretching his legs out in front of
him. 'Peace and quiet, not a sound to be heard outside.
Mind you,' he went on, grinning, 'I'll bet those damn
birds and their wretched dawn chorus will have me
awake at some ungodly hour in the morning.'

'It'll be noisy well before that if this storm comes,'
Lynette pointed out. 'I wish it would break, though, it
might get a little cooler then.'

Jill was lifting her brandy glass to her lips as Lynette
spoke, intending only to pretend to drink in the hope of
finding a quiet moment when she could dispose of the
brandy as she had done the wine, but the talk of the
storm agitated her so that, unthinkingly, she swallowed
far more than she had planned. The fiery liquid burned
the back of her throat so that she choked, her eyes
watering painfully.

'All right, Jill?' Luke enquired blandly.

Sparks flashed in her mind. She was beginning to feel

distinctly harassed; she wished he would stop watching her all the time.

'Fine, thanks,' she managed sharply and a little hoarsely.

'Take it steady if you're not used to it.'

His advice was reasonable, as was his tone, but his words fanned the flame of resentment inside her and her fingers tightened angrily on her glass.

'If I want your advice I'll ask for it!' she snapped, heedless of the Kellys' astonished glances. Luke sighed his exasperation.

'For God's sake, Jill, grow up,' he said irritably, his words guaranteed to add fuel to the fire of Jill's anger. They were glaring at each other now across the room, oblivious of anyone else.

'Don't talk to me like that!' Jill shouted furiously. 'What gives you the right to sit there and——'

'Jill——' Luke began quietly, but if he said any more she didn't hear it, for the room had suddenly begun to sway alarmingly. Hastily she got to her feet, but that only made things so much worse. Through a blur she saw Luke's expression change, saw his swift movement out of his chair.

She couldn't let him help her; that would be the final indignity. Instinctively she held out her hands to fend him off and with a thickly muttered, 'Excuse me', ran from the room, blundering painfully into the settee as she fled. To her relief no one came after her as she dashed to the cloakroom just off the hall. That, at least, she had been spared.

Some time later, she had no idea how long, the appalling rolling of the floor began to ease and after splashing her face vigorously with cold water she started to feel relatively human again. What she needed now, she decided, taking slow, deep breaths to calm herself,

was to reach the safety of her room before anyone saw
her.

Cautiously she peered out from her refuge, relieved to
find that the door to the garden room was closed and the
hall was empty. Moving as quietly as possible on her
unsteady legs, her eyes fixed firmly on the ground, she
hurried along the hallway. Dimly she was aware of the
sound of a door opening, but didn't register the
direction from which it came. Her head bent, not
looking where she was going, she made her way to the
stairs—and crashed headlong into someone standing at
the foot of them.

Knocked off balance, she reeled and almost fell, but
strong hands supported her and a mild voice somewhere
above her head said, 'I thought you were in bed.'

Blinking hard to clear her blurred vision, she looked
up to see Luke's blue eyes regarding her, their
expression unreadable.

'I—was just going,' she said miserably, dropping her
eyes again, unable to meet his steady, searching gaze.
She flinched under Luke's silent scrutiny, knowing she
must look a mess with streaks of mascara on her cheeks
and the make-up Lynette had so carefully applied
smudged everywhere. Miserably she raised a hand to
wipe her face, a childlike gesture that only made matters
worse and which suddenly and inexplicably altered the
expression on Luke's face.

The mildly tolerant condescension vanished, his eyes
darkening perceptibly as he reached out and pulled her
to him roughly. Holding her tight against the hard
length of his body, he forced her head up, one hand
under her chin, and brought his mouth down hard on
hers. His kiss bruised her lips savagely, but she was
oblivious to the pain, her mind too numb to form any
thought of resistance as she returned the kiss with all the
force of the need and longing that seared through her.

On a sigh of total surrender she murmured Luke's name against his lips, the soft sound turning into a cry of shock and pain as she felt him stiffen and withdraw from her. Bringing his head up with an abruptness that threatened to tear her in two, he pushed her away from him.

'I think you'd better go to bed,' he said in a voice that was thick and harsh. 'And for God's sake wash that muck off your face!'

Her head reeling with the pain of his rejection, Jill forced her legs to carry her upstairs, holding tightly to the banister for support. There was just a raw wound where her heart should be and tears of loss for the devastation of all her dreams burned in her eyes. She could not delude herself any longer; there was no hope for her or for anyone where Luke was concerned. That kiss had left her feeling used. To him she was just another conquest, as meaningless as all the ones before Marianne, but the worst pain came from remembering what Paul had told her, knowing that Marianne was the only woman who had captured Luke's love. She was still there too, always in his mind, and there was no room in his heart for anyone else.

When the storm that had been threatening all evening finally broke, it did so with a suddenness and a ferocity that penetrated even the unnaturally heavy sleep into which Jill had fallen, jerking her wide awake so that she sat up in bed, bewildered and confused, wondering what had disturbed her. She didn't have to wonder long; a second flash of lightning followed swiftly on the first, succeeded in its turn by a crash of thunder that made her dive under the bedclothes. Buried in a warm cave of blankets, shielded from the rage of the storm, she tried desperately to think. She couldn't bear to be alone, but there was no one she could turn to. It was after one o'clock; everyone was probably in bed and she could hardly drag Jenky or the Kellys from their sleep just to keep her company in her childish fear—and as for Luke, the idea was unthinkable. Perhaps a warm, milky drink might help.

Cautiously she made her way downstairs, concentrating on the thought of how soothing a warm drink would be in an effort to keep her mind off the violent forces that seemed to be lashing the house, their fury aggravated by Stoneroyd's exposed position. She had almost reached the bottom of the staircase when a voice sounded suddenly out of the darkness.

'All right, Lady Macbeth, what the hell are you doing now?'

# CHAPTER TWELVE

TAKEN completely by surprise, Jill turned, startled, missed her footing, slipped and bumped her way down the remaining three stairs, to land in an undignified heap on the floor. At first she could not tell where the voice had come from, but then another brilliant flash of lightning illuminated an all-too-familiar tall figure lounging in the open doorway of the garden room.

'Well?' demanded Luke as she tried to gather her scattered thoughts.

'I—wanted something to drink,' she said shakily, getting slowly to her feet, holding on the banister for support.

'I should have thought you'd had enough already,' was the callous response.

'I meant milk or something—to make me sleep!' she snapped. Her nerves were already strung to breaking point, she couldn't take any more of his taunts. 'I didn't know anyone was still up,' she added stiffly. 'But you needn't worry, I won't disturb you—I can manage perfectly.'

Drawing herself up, she set off down the unlit corridor, misjudged the distance and banged painfully into the wall, reeling back with a sharp cry.

'For someone who can manage perfectly, you don't seem to be making too good a job of it,' Luke drawled sardonically as he straightened up. 'I think I'd better see to this drink for you.'

'I said I can manage!' Jill declared indignantly, wanting to refute the implication that she was still affected by the wine she had drunk.

'Yes, but I think I would manage rather better,' Luke said, coming to her side. With firm hands he turned her round so that she was once more facing the stairs. 'You go back to your room and I'll bring you some milk,' he said with a careful patience that had her gritting her teeth against the irritation that welled up inside her. 'Think you can negotiate the stairs without breaking your neck?'

'I should have thought you'd like to see me do just that!' she responded tartly.

'And have a genuine body in the basement? Your Mrs Dawson would love that.' Jill couldn't see his face in the darkness, but there was no mistaking the amusement warming his voice. 'Let's have no more argument—off you go or I'll carry you up myself.'

The subtle change in his tone warned her that this time he was not joking, and deciding it was better not to risk provoking him to carry out his threat, she pulled away from his restraining grasp and headed back up the stairs.

In her room she perched nervously on the edge of the bed, unable to make herself get into it in spite of the fact that she was now beginning to feel distinctly chilled. Remembering Luke's kiss earlier, she felt that to be *in* bed, waiting for him, seemed to imply something she had no intention of allowing him to think.

The storm had lessened slightly, grumbling sullenly somewhere in the distance, but now that she was alone again the fear that had been pushed to the back of her mind by the confrontation with Luke returned in full force. She hoped he wouldn't be long; even his disturbing company was preferable to being alone.

He came at last, carrying a mug full of milk. Seeing him in the light for the first time, Jill realised with a shock that his hair and clothes were wet, the light material of his shirt clinging damply to the firm muscles of his chest in a way that made her heart lurch betrayingly. Now, when she was least able to cope with it, she was once more made forcefully aware of the sheer physical impact of his presence.

'You're soaked!' she said jerkily, praying that he would believe the unevenness of her voice to be the result of surprise, though her heart was beating so frantically that she felt sure he must hear its pounding in the stillness of the night.

'A bit,' he agreed laconically. 'I couldn't sleep either, so I took the dogs out. I got caught in the storm.'

'You should get out of those wet things.' Jill's tone was reproving.

'And you should be in bed,' he countered drily. 'Neither of which is exactly a proper suggestion, considering the time and our surroundings. Perhaps we could come to some arrangement?'

'What are you suggesting?' asked Jill, half indignantly, half fearfully.

'I'm suggesting nothing beyond the fact that you'd be more comfortable if you got into bed. And while you do that I'll fetch a towel.'

As soon as he had left the room Jill scrambled hurriedly into bed, pulling the blankets closely round her. A gleam in Luke's eyes, the trace of mockery in his voice had made her suddenly very much aware of the fact that the flimsy cotton of her nightdress provided little protection from that appraising dark blue gaze. She was huddled in bed, the mug in her hands, when he returned, rubbing his wet hair with a towel. He paused in the doorway to regard her with an amused smile hovering around the corners of his hard mouth.

'I was right about the duckling,' he said, a thread of laughter warming his voice. 'That's just what you look like, a fluffy baby duckling in its nest, scared to move in case the sky falls on its head.'

'You've got your stories muddled,' retorted Jill. 'It was Chicken Licken who thought the sky had fallen down.'

Luke's chuckle was a warm, good-humoured sound. 'I suppose I asked for that,' he said, lowering himself into a chair beside the bed. 'I should have known better than to quote fairy stories at a children's librarian.'

'Yes, you should.' Jill even managed a smile, relaxing slightly at the recognition of the easy, teasing mood that appeared so rarely.

Suddenly his expression changed subtly as he leaned towards her slightly. 'You gave me quite a fright, appearing on the stairs like that. I didn't expect you to surface before morning—if then. You must have a pretty strong head after all.'

She scowled, hating him for reminding her of her foolish behaviour earlier, but the scowl vanished immediately, to be replaced by a disturbed, apprehensive expression when she looked into Luke's eyes and found them hard and darkly suspicious.

'Why *were* you wandering around the house half-naked?'

'I told you—I wanted a drink! And I wasn't—what you said.'

'Near enough,' he drawled satirically. 'Hardly the right attire for a midnight feast, if that was really what you were after.'

Jill's hands clenched around her mug. Well aware of just what he was implying, she found the temptation to fling it and its contents at his head almost irresistible.

'I certainly wasn't looking for you, if that's what you're thinking! God, you're so arrogant! I suppose you think no woman can resist you!'

'There wasn't much resisting going on earlier, if I remember rightly,' Luke reminded her softly, bringing a rush of hot, embarrassed colour to her cheeks. For one brief, foolish moment she had let her feelings show and by doing so had left herself wide-open and vulnerable to any move he might make. She had no hope of any return of feeling from him, but for very different reasons from the ones that had made her keep her distance before, and she didn't know which was worse, to believe that Luke was a heartless, unfaithful womaniser or to know that he had cared for his wife so deeply that no other woman could ever take her place.

'If you must know, I was frightened by the storm,' she muttered through clenched teeth, keeping her voice even only by a supreme effort of will. 'And as for my behaviour earlier, you know perfectly well I'd had too much to drink.'

'*In vino veritas*,' murmured Luke, almost to himself.

At that moment the storm, which had been nothing but a low muttering far away, suddenly returned in full force with a brilliant flash of lightning followed almost immediately by a violent crash of thunder practically overhead, making Jill shrink back on the bed, spilling the milk all over the blankets. Luke's reaction was immediate. In one swift, lithe momement he was out of his chair, taking the mug from her trembling hands and placing it safely on the bedside cabinet.

'You *are* scared, aren't you?' he said more gently, sitting on the bed beside her and taking her hand in his. Then as another flash of lightning lit up the room and he saw her start of fear his arm came round her shoulders, warm and strong and infinitely comforting. 'It's all right, Jill,' he soothed in the same voice he had used when Danny had had his nightmare. 'You're quite safe.'

And she did feel safe, wonderfully, reassuringly safe. When the lightning came again she buried her face in Luke's shoulder where his shirt was still slightly damp, the warmth of his skin reaching her through the thin material, and felt his hand come up to hold her head. His fingers gently stroked her hair as he murmured words she couldn't quite hear through the noise of the thunder. But it didn't matter; she felt safe, protected, relaxed at last. If this kindly gentleness was all that he could give her, then she'd take it and be glad of it.

But even as her mind formed the thought every sense was reacting violently to the touch of his hands, the sound of the steady beat of his heart beneath her cheek, the scent of his body setting her nerves quivering so that she knew with a stab of despair that it could *never* be enough. She wanted so much more than this, so that when Luke moved carefully, easing his uncomfortable position, she clutched at his arm to restrain him with a small, wordless cry of protest.

'Don't worry, little one,' he said quietly, misinterpreting her reaction. 'I won't leave you, I promise. I'll stay till it's all over, till you're asleep. But I'm sure this could be arranged a little better.'

Gently putting her from him, he moved on to the bed beside her, leaning back against the pillows.

'That's more like it,' he murmured softly, holding out his arms to her.

For a long, silent second Jill hesitated, torn between a longing to be in his arms once more and the knowledge that it would only bring her pain to be there when it meant nothing at all to Luke. Then a further crash of thunder decided things for her, and she moved close up against him, her head pillowed on his chest, the strength of his arms coming tightly round her.

Immediately it was as if the storm did not exist. She was only conscious of how right it felt to be there, the most natural thing in the world and the most perfect, to feel the warmth of his body beside her, his hand caressing her face, his cheek against her hair. Her need of him went deeper than any fear or sense of self-preservation, and instinctively she nestled closer, like a small animal seeking refuge. She murmured his name, all the love and longing she had ever felt expressed in that single syllable, and heard his swiftly indrawn breath as the arm around her shoulders tightened convulsively.

He moved then, rolling her on to her back, her head resting on the pillows, and lay half across her, a hand on either side of her as he studied her face, his eyes darkly intent. Then very slowly he lowered his head and brushed a soft, gentle kiss over her forehead.

Jill felt as if her bones were melting, as if she was sinking into the deep softness of the bed, her whole body limp with pleasure. Why did I ever think it would hurt to love him? she wondered dreamily. Something as wonderful as this could never hurt, and whatever happened it was enough to have had this moment. Her blood glowed in her veins, suffusing her face with delicate colour as she reached up a hand to touch his cheek.

'I want you,' she whispered enticingly. 'I want you to love me, Luke.'

A frown creased the space between the dark eyes and something strangely like pain showed in their depths. When he spoke, his voice was husky as if his throat was painfully dry.

'You don't know what you're talking about, Jill. I think you must still be a little drunk.'

His words were like a dash of icy water in her face. She gasped faintly and tried to sit up, struggling vainly against the imprisoning weight of his body.

'I *do* know what I'm saying!' she protested vehemently. 'And I'm pefectly sober now!' Though that was not exactly true, she admitted privately to herself. The sensations she had been experiencing were far more intoxicating than any wine.

Luke raised himself slightly, leaning on his elbows and looked searchingly into her face, flushed and bright-eyed on the pillows. His blue eyes were wary beneath their half-closed lids.

'I still think you'd be better trying to sleep,' he said carefully, 'before anything happens that we'll both regret in the morning.'

'I won't regret a thing!' she assured him, swept away beyond thought of anything other than this moment. 'Not for a second; not for the rest of my life!'

'Jill!' Her name was a groan as Luke rolled away from her to lie on his back beside her, his eyes closed.

Very slowly she sat up, feeling bewildered and rejected. Wasn't this what he'd wanted? That kiss had made her so very sure that it was. He lay very still, keeping his eyes tightly closed. His still damp hair was ruffled, falling in soft disorder over his face, and she reached out a tentative hand to smooth it back into place. The feel of its softness beneath her fingertips was exhilarating, sending a thrill like a burning electric current running up her arm, a shock so intense that she felt sure Luke must sense it too, though he did not react but lay still and silent as before as she twisted a silver-gilt strand of hair around her fingers, glorying in the freedom to touch him at last.

Emboldened by the fact that Luke did nothing to stop her, she trailed her fingers down his face, stroking the closed lids, the lean cheeks, and traced the outline of his lips with a gentle forefinger before moving down the strong column of his throat to the open neck of his shirt. But as her fingers slid under his collar, feeling the warmth of his skin beneath the silk, his hand suddenly closed around her wrist and his eyes opened, staring directly into hers. The sudden flash of raw emotion she saw there held her motionless, unable to look away.

'Damn you, Jill!' His voice was low and husky. 'You have to know what you're doing to me!'

She couldn't be unaware of what he meant. Held so

close to him, she could feel his need of her, a need that was mirrored in her own body, the ache in the pit of her stomach growing to a clamorous desire that she had no words to express. But she didn't have a chance to say anything, because at that moment Luke raised his arm and, hooking it around her neck, pulled her down on top of him and kissed her hard.

This time it was so very, very different from that earlier kiss that had abused rather than caressed her lips. Luke's mouth was warm and devastatingly sensuous as it explored hers, coaxing it open with his tongue. Fire flickered in her veins, a warm golden heat that followed the path of his hands as they slid down her back, so strong and yet so gentle. Her body felt soft as wax, pliant against his hardness as she abandoned herself to her feelings, clinging to him with all her strength, her mouth softening under his.

When they finally parted Luke's breathing was ragged and uneven. Less gently than before he rolled Jill on to her back, covering her face with butterfly-soft kisses which tantalised and tormented her by their brief sweetness.

'Luke——' she sighed. 'I——'

But he stopped her mouth with his, apparently oblivious to the fact that her nails were digging into his shoulders as she arched her body towards his, and his hand moved from her face to ease the soft material of her nightdress down from her shoulders.

At the touch of his fingers on her skin Jill could not suppress a shudder of delight, and when he pressed his lips to the soft breast his impatient hands had exposed she moaned aloud, his name a cry of joy in the silence of the night. She wanted this so much, her whole body one ache of longing so that she was aware of nothing beyond it, and she missed Luke's sudden stiffening, did not notice that anything was wrong until with a violent twisting movement he flung himself from her and off the bed to stand towering above her, his height and strength so threatening that instinctively she shrank back against the pillows, one nerveless hand clutching tightly at the front of her nightdress, pulling it back up over her nakedness. Her mind was just a haze of pain and loss, her body feeling cold and unreal, bereft of the warm comfort of his hard strength. She knew Luke was watching her, but she could not meet his eyes, not yet.

'Jill.' His voice was harsh. 'Look at me.'

Still she kept her head turned away. With an impatient sound in his throat he came to sit on the bed, pulling her face round so that he could see her eyes.

'I said, look at me!'

The long, searching look he gave her unnerved her completely. She felt desolated, destroyed by his rejection, and in the mixture of violent emotions that were etched into his face it was impossible to find one that was clear enough to tell her exactly what he was thinking. His eyes went to her hands, still clutching at her nightdress, then back to her face, and they were as dark and bleak as a winter sky at night.

'This has to stop,' he told her in a low, forceful voice. 'It could get dangerous if it doesn't.'

'Dangerous?' Jill's voice shook on the word. 'I don't understand. I thought you wanted——'

'*Wanted!* God, Jill!' he said huskily. 'Can't you see this is exactly what I *didn't* want to happen?'

'But why?' It was a cry of pain. 'Tell me why! Is—is it because of Marianne?'

He didn't have to speak; his reaction told her she had hit home. His face whitened and his head went back as if he had been struck.

'Yes,' he said flatly. 'Because of Marianne. So now do you see why this has to stop?'

Jill nodded silently. She couldn't help but see what he

meant, and really, she had known it all along, but
foolishly, in her need for him, she had allowed herself to
forget, to pretend she did not know.

'I see,' she said unhappily, and then, because there
seemed nothing else to do, she slid down in the bed,
pulling the blankets up around her. 'I think I'd better go
to sleep.'

'That might be best.' Luke's reply was almost
drowned by the roar of the thunder, and she smiled
wryly to herself at the thought that, in the confusion of
feelings that had swept through her, she had had no time
or opportunity to feel afraid of the storm. Perhaps not in
quite the same way as throwing an imaginary crocodile
out of the window, but Luke had dealt with her own
private nightmare as effectively as he had dealt with
Danny's. The memory of the way Luke had sung a
lullaby to his son brought the question that had been
nagging at her all evening to the surface of her mind.

'Luke,' she said impulsively, 'why are you bringing
all that musical equipment up to Stoneroyd?'

His eyes were very dark but clear and open and
unshadowed as he answered her. 'Isn't it obvious? After
all, it's what you've been telling me I should do ever
since you arrived. You said I should leave the company
to run itself,' he went on as she shook her head in
confusion. 'You wanted me to spend more time at
Stoneroyd and——'

Jill didn't give him time to finish, the importance of
what he was saying suddenly dawning on her like a light
being switched on in a darkened room. She sat up
swiftly.

'You're going to start writing music again!' Her voice
was breathless with stunned delight. 'But why? I
mean—what made you——' She stumbled over her
words, unable to get them out, but then she recognised
the look on his face as the one that had been there in the

car after the picnic and again on her birthday when he had come into the room to find herself and Danny singing their hearts out. 'Danny! It's Danny that changed your mind! No?' she finished uncertainly as Luke shook his head.

'It *was* hearing Danny sing that reminded me of how much music had once meant to me, but it was you who taught him to sing like that. *You* brought music back into my life.'

'I did?' She *had* given him something—something that meant a great deal to him. Tears of joy sprang into her eyes, and the effect of them on Luke was dramatic. Shock, concern and something very close to delight flickered across his face in quick succession and he leaned forward to touch her wet cheek with a gentle forefinger.

'Tears, Jill?' he questioned huskily. 'Why are you crying?'

'Because I'm so happy for you!' Jill told him honestly. 'You'd lost your music, but now you've got it back, and it's—wonderful!'

The last word came out on a gasp as Luke's soft touch turned into a deliberate caress, the palm of his hand smoothing over the delicate skin of her cheek and sliding into her hair at the nape of her neck.

'It matters that much to you?' he said on a note of hesitant disbelief that, in her longing to erase it from his voice, left her with no thought of hiding anything from him.

'It means everything to me,' she assured him, sincerity ringing in her voice. 'Music is such a vital part of you, a part that died with——' She dropped her eyes suddenly, disturbed by the intent, searching look that was fixed on her face as if Luke wanted to draw out her most private thoughts. 'With Marianne,' she added shakily.

'Marianne.' Luke's voice was low and his thumb moved in slow sensuous circles over the taut muscles of her neck. 'Marianne hated my work, she was jealous of the time I gave to it, she didn't even want to hear the music I wrote. So I came to separate it from my home life, keep the two worlds totally apart, until there was no pleasure in composing any more—it was just a job I did. I lost the inspiration and in the end stopped writing music at all. Danny's grown up not knowing what I used to do. The only music he thinks I know are the lullabies I used to sing when he was little.'

'The sleepytown song,' Jill murmured shakily. His gentle massaging of her neck was affecting the rest of her body, her blood glowed with a sensual warmth, a pulse beat strongly in her throat and her mind was slightly hazy with the sheer joy of his touch. Luke smiled slightly.

'The sleepytown song,' he confirmed softly, wryly. 'My only composition in five years. But when I heard you and Danny singing just for the joy of it, it reminded me of what I'd lost. I wanted that joy back again—I found I couldn't concentrate on my work, my mind was buzzing with ideas.' His hand slid from her neck to her shoulders, its warmth seeming to scorch a path on her sensitive skin as he leaned towards her, coming so close that his face was only inches away from her. 'So you see, you gave me back what Marianne took away.'

She had never seen eyes of such an intense blue before, she thought vaguely. They were so deep and dark she felt she might drown in them, and they said everything he hadn't put into words, the hard control of only minutes before vanished completely as he silently asked the question that he couldn't frame but which reached her on the sensitive antennae of instinct as clearly as if he had spoken out loud. And she knew what her answer would be, felt the sense of rightness and completeness flood through her so that she was sure that her feelings must be written clearly on her face, open and unconcealed for him to read. But still she had to speak, because there was something very important she had to say.

'Luke,' she said softly, and saw his eyes drop to her moving lips, the tiny movement sending her heart into a slow, heavy pounding that drowned the sound of the thunder once and for all. 'Luke—I'm not Marianne.'

His lips were so close now that she could feel the warmth of his breath on her cheek as he sighed.

'I know,' he whispered just before he kissed her. 'Dear God, I know.'

# CHAPTER THIRTEEN

IN THE still quiet that followed the end of the storm Jill woke and lay with her eyes closed, listening to the busy sounds of the birds outside. The dawn chorus, she thought, and wondered if, in his room on the other side of the house, Paul too had been woken by the birds as he had predicted. Then, as she stretched lazily, she became aware of an unusual, languorous heaviness about her body, and in particular one unexpected weight across her waist. She reached out to discover what it was and, finding a familiar long-fingered hand with a thick ring on one finger, smiled in delighted recollection of the pleasure that hand had given her earlier.

Moving as carefully as possible so as not to disturb Luke, she twisted round until she could see his face. In sleep he looked younger, more vulnerable somehow and very much like Danny, the heavy lids tightly closed over those midnight-blue eyes and his hair falling in soft disarray over his forehead. For some time she was content to lie there and watch him, keeping very still for fear the slightest movement would wake him and the peaceful, relaxed mood would be spoiled, because, in spite of the passion that had flared between them during the night, she still didn't know if, when he woke in the cold light of day, that withdrawn, distant look would come into his eyes and he would be further away from her than ever. If this was just a temporary, fleeting idyll of happiness then, for this short time at least, she wanted to enjoy simply having him close to her.

Luke stirred slightly in his sleep and moved closer, his hand reaching out to her. When it touched her cheek he sighed faintly, his warm breath fanning her cheek as he

172

relaxed again to lie with his face in her hair. His movement meant that his body no longer hid the clock from her sight, and as she mechanically noted the time Jill felt a sudden flash of panic, remembering Danny. In an hour or so the little boy would wake and come into the room, seeking her, and she knew that if he found Luke and herself together it would not be long before everyone else in the house knew that Luke had spent the night in her bed. Feeling instinctively that that was something Luke would not want, Jill felt she had to do something to prevent it happening.

Reluctantly and moving with infinite care, she inched away from him to the side of the bed, then froze as he stirred again as if sensing the emptiness beside him.

'Love?' he murmured questioningly, his eyes still closed.

Jill touched his hands gently. 'I'm here,' she said softly, hoping it was the response he wanted. He made a small, contented sound in his throat and relaxed into sleep again. She felt her eyes burn with unshed tears as she watched him, wondering just who, in his half-awake state, he had thought was with him. Was it Marianne who even now still haunted his dreams? In the night he had told her that he knew she was not his wife, he had made love to her as herself, not as a substitute for any other woman, but had that been just a fleeting desire, born out of a passing need or something stronger? She didn't know, and because of Danny she couldn't stay to see his reaction when he woke, in spite of the fact that those first few unguarded seconds would tell her all she needed to know. Pausing only to pull the blankets she had disturbed up around the sleeping man, she crept out of the room and crossed the landing to where Danny slept.

The little boy did not wake as she slid into the bed beside him but, sensing her presence, snuggled close to her in a way that reminded Jill unbearably of his father.

She slipped her arms around the child and held him tight while tears of doubt and fear slid from under her lids and seeped into the pillow.

Jill was in the garden with Danny when Jenky came to find her. She was surprised to see the housekeeper making her way across the lawn towards her, it was some time before lunch was due and she could think of no other reason why the older woman should seek her out. But when she saw the worried, shocked look on the housekeeper's face she knew it was no casual chat she had come for.

'What is it, Jenky?' she asked, concern sharpening her voice, then, seeing the housekeeper's uneasy glance towards the study, she went on, 'Is it Luke?'

Slowly Jenky nodded. 'He sent me to fetch you—he wants to see you—immediately, he said.' Her shaken tone revealed exactly *how* he had said it too, and Jill didn't need the housekeeper's anxious, 'He's in a terrible temper,' to tell her the mood Luke was in. 'You'd better go—I'll look after Danny. Oh, Jill, what have you done?'

What *had* she done? No answer came to Jill as she forced her legs to cross the hall towards the study door. All she could think of was the events of the night, but none of that seemed to explain Luke's sudden anger—unless he felt this way because she had crept away while he still slept.

Her mind went back over the time since Danny had woken. She had been intensely grateful for his surprised but unquestioning acceptance of her presence in his bed, if he had demanded an explanation she had no idea what answer she could have given. But from the moment he had stirred she was back in the busy routine of his day and had no time to think of anything else.

There had been a difficult moment when she had realised that she would have to go into her own room to

collect her clothes, but when she had peeped round the
half-open door it was to find that Luke had gone and the
bedroom was empty, her bed neatly made as if the night
had never been. But Jill knew it had and that at some
time she would have to face Luke and judge from his
reaction how he felt. When she considered that moment
in anticipation she had thought he might be distant,
indifferent, perhaps even a little embarrassed, had
believed he might tell her it had all been a mistake, that it
meant nothing at all—but anger she had never expected.

The study door was partly open and it swung away
from her as she tried to knock, leaving her no alternative
but to move uncertainly into the room, stopping dead
suddenly as she was blinded by the blaze of sunlight
streaming through the window directly into her eyes.
For a moment she blinked dazedly, then at one corner of
the glare a dark shape moved and her head swung round
so that she could see him clearly.

'Luke?' Her voice was hesitant and uneven.

'Luke,' a mocking snarl echoed her use of his name.
'Is that all you can manage? Surely you and your friend
cooked up something more imaginative than that!'

The colour fled from Jill's cheeks at his tone and she
frowned her bewilderment. 'I—I don't understand.'

'No?' Luke questioned harshly. 'You're not trying to
tell me you don't know—or did your boyfriend break the
story before you were ready? You couldn't have got the
news of last night's little triumph to him in time for
today's first editions, so I reckon he must have jumped
the gun a bit. I expect you thought he'd give you time to
get well clear before he printed his little scoop—
unluckily for you he didn't.'

'Luke, what are you talking about?' she cried
desperately. 'You're not making any sense at all!'

'What am I talking about?' He moved suddenly,
flinging something on to the desk that stood between
them. 'That's what I'm talking about!' One lean finger

stabbed viciously at the black-printed sheet. 'Now tell me you know nothing about it!'

Numbly Jill stared at the open newspaper, recognising it as one of the more popular, scandal-spreading dailies. From the page the headline leapt out at her, 'New Romance for Recluse of Stoneroyd', and beside it a photograph of Luke and Marianne with one of herself taken two years before and obtained from God knew where. But worst of all and most damning, in Luke's eyes at least, was the name of the author of the report—Tony Atkins.

'But I didn't——' she cried despairingly. 'I couldn't——'

'No?' Luke's voice cut in on her harshly. 'That's your friend, isn't it?'

'No! I mean—I *know* him, but——'

But the words died on her lips as she saw Luke's face and knew that that tiny hesitation had condemned her.

'You knew how I felt about publicity!' He flung the words at her ashen face. 'I trusted you, damn you!' Jill flinched away as his voice rose to a shout.

'Luke——' she tried again, beseechingly, but he ignored her.

'God, when I think——' He cut himself off sharply and when he spoke again his voice was coldly controlled, his words falling into the silence like slivers of ice. 'You were employed here on the condition that you could be trusted, you have broken that trust. I would appreciate it if you would pack your bags and leave this house immediately—without speaking to Danny or anyone else.'

Something died inside Jill as she heard that hard, cold voice. All her half-formed dreams and hopes which she had barely begun to allow herself to feel shrivelled into ashes in her heart. She wanted to cry out, to protest at the injustice of his suspicions, but her throat seemed to have closed up and no words would come. The eyes

Luke turned on her were hard as steel and every bit as impenetrable, all feeling burned away in his anger.

'What are you waiting for?' he snarled. 'Your money? I don't have it here—I'll send what you've earned on to you.'

'I——' Jill longed to contradict his suggestion vehemently, but even as she opened her mouth she saw his tightly-clenched fists, his knuckles showing white from the pressure, and heard again in her mind his threatening promise to make her wish she had never seen Stoneroyd, and as Luke took one step towards her her control broke completely and she turned and fled from the room.

She was in her bedroom when the doorbell rang. She heard her mother's footsteps going down the hall and briefly but uninterestedly wonderd who it might be calling so early. Her father had only just left for work and she and her mother were just straightening round before they began on the day's tasks.

One of those tasks, Jill reflected drearily, would be to call in at the local library and search through the papers for any jobs for which she could apply.

She sighed unhappily. How desperately she wanted a job—and preferably one as far away from Stoneroyd as possible—only she knew. It was her only chance of starting again, beginning a new life. She could only hope a move to some other part of the country would enable her to forget Luke, or at least help her memories of him to grow dim, something that would never happen as long as she remained at Burnbridge.

The thought of Stoneroyd was almost more than she could bear. The memory of her hasty flight from the house was infinitely painful. She had hated leaving Danny so abruptly, without even time to say goodbye, but if she had risked defying Luke's order not to see his son she would probably have had to face his father too, and that she knew she could not have borne.

'Jill!' It was her mother's voice calling up the stairs, a strangely apprehensive note in it. 'There's a gentleman to see you, he says it's about a job.'

A job? Jill frowned, puzzled. In the three weeks since she had left Stoneroyd there had only been one position that had attracted her, and only that morning she had received a formal 'regret to inform you that on this occasion your application has not been successful' letter in the post. Deep down, she knew she didn't really want any job except perhaps the one looking after Luke's library that Paul had suggested—determinedly she squashed down that thought. That was one job she could never accept even if it were offered, which she knew in her heart it would never be.

With an effort she dragged her mind back to the present. Her clothes, scruffy jeans and an old, faded T-shirt, weren't exactly suitable for a possible interview, and when she checked her hair in the mirror the face that looked back at her appeared thinner, more fragile, her cheeks pale and her eyes heavy after endless sleepless nights and far too many tears. Her parents had been too tactful to comment on her sudden return home, but just lately her mother had made one or two pointed remarks about the way she looked.

But who could this unexpected caller be? Butterflies of apprehension began to flutter in Jill's stomach as she ran downstairs. Her mother was clattering cups and saucers in the kitchen, clearly the gentleman, whoever he was, had been offered coffee, but there wasn't time to snatch a few words, ask just who was waiting for her. A little breathless from the suddenness of everything, Jill opened the living-room door and went in.

'I'm sorry to keep you . . .' The words died on her lips as she took in the tall figure standing by the window. 'You!' she gasped, all colour leaving her face.

'Me,' Luke agreed flatly. 'I'm sorry if you were

expecting someone else.'

Jill could only shake her head, too stunned to speak. No wonder her mother had sounded nervous! The appearance of Luke Garrett on her doorstep, the imposing car parked outside, would have sent the quiet, shy Mrs Carpenter into a flurry of panic. With an effort Jill pulled herself together, gathering her disordered thoughts.

'Would you like to sit down?' she asked, keeping her tone carefully polite. When Luke's only response was a silent shake of his head she decided against sitting down herself. His height made her feel too vulnerable as it was, without the added disadvantage of being seated. She wished her mother would hurry with the coffee.

Luke was lighting a cigarette; he appeared to be having trouble with his lighter, taking several attempts to produce a flame, and this uncharacteristic awkwardness made Jill study him more closely. He looked pale too and as tired as herself, the dark blue of his shirt and trousers accentuating his pallor and making the lines on his face seem more deeply etched than ever.

'How's everyone at Stoneroyd?' she asked awkwardly, simply for something to say.

'Just fine,' was Luke's response, but his bitterly cynical tone belied the easy words. 'Danny's desolate and wanders round like a lost soul, refusing to be comforted. Lynette spends most of her time telling me what a fool I've been. Every photographer under the sun seems to want a picture of me or Stoneroyd or both—and your friend Atkins is pestering me for another "exclusive" at every opportunity—but otherwise things are quite normal.'

'Tony Atkins is *not* my friend!' Jill cried sharply, and he turned blank, dull eyes towards her.

'No,' he said slowly. 'He told me. I apologise for doubting you.'

The removal of that particular point of conflict should

have brought some release from the tension that held every muscle strained tight, but she was too hypersensitive to Luke to feel any relief. His apology had been so distant, so formally phrased, that it barely touched her. She recognised his mood and her heart sank despondently. The barriers were up between them as clearly as if she could actually see them around him, with a sign saying 'Keep Out' where no one could miss it.

'Mum said you'd come about a job for me, but she must have been mistaken.'

'No.' Luke shook his head. 'There's no mistake. That's what I told her.'

'*You're* offering me a job?' It came out on a shaken gasp.

His mouth twisted wryly. 'I have no choice, Danny's making my life hell. He won't eat, he won't sleep. He needs you, Jill. I came to ask if you'd come back, look after him on a permanent basis. I realise it's a lot to ask,' he went on as she stared at him in stunned, incredulous astonishment.

'You'd be wasting your training, but I'd pay you whatever you'd get as a librarian—you'd not lose by it that way.'

Deep inside a tiny, faint hope began to stir. If she and Luke had more time together, now that he knew the truth about the newspaper report, then—— Ruthlessly Jill crushed the thought down again. All the time in the world wouldn't help. Luke had been offering her nothing more than a purely business proposition. If she went to Stoneroyd now, it would be a step backwards, several steps, destroying the hard work she had already put in just to get this far without breaking down. Even for Danny's sake she couldn't sacrifice herself like that.

'I'm afraid I have to say no,' she told him as calmly as she could manage, trying desperately to keep the pain from her voice. 'I'm desperately sorry to upset Danny like this, but I do have my own life to think of. As a matter of fact,' behind her back she crossed her fingers against the white lie, 'I had a letter about a job only this morning.'

'I see.' Luke's voice gave away even less than his expression. 'I rather thought that would be your answer. I'm glad you've found a job, you'll be able to enjoy that independence you so value.' He was reaching into his pocket as he spoke and so he missed the way Jill bit her lip hard at his reminder of her own unthinking words. If he only knew how willingly she would exchange that independence for one word of love! 'This should tide you over until you get your first salary.'

She took the cheque he held out to her in a hand that was distinctly unsteady. The figures on it blurred before her eyes as she fought against the tears that threatened at the way his actions reinforced the fact that he had come solely on business, any more personal contact between them might never have existed.

'But this isn't right! You don't owe me so much!'

Luke's shrug was dismissive. 'I employed you for three months, I've paid you for three months,' he said indifferently.

'But I didn't work the full three months!' she protested. 'And you've already paid me something. You only owe me for four weeks or so, I won't take the rest.'

'I can afford it.'

'No!' She thrust the cheque back at him, heedless of the way his face had darkened ominously. He moved suddenly, not to take the cheque, but to force it back into her hand and close her fingers over it, his own hand on top of hers, crushing it in a painful grip.

'Take it!' he muttered through clenched teeth. 'It's the least I can do.'

The touch of his hands on hers, reminding her of the pleasure they could give, the feelings they had aroused in her almost defeated her and she had to force herself to speak.

'I don't want your money, Luke!'

Suddenly, blindingly, she realised what he was doing. He wanted to make up to her for the way he had treated her, and he believed that the extra money would ease the wounds he had inflicted on her heart. The thought stabbed like a white-hot knife.

'Is your conscience troubling you because you made love to me?' she demanded, all the hurt she had felt in the last few weeks ringing in her voice. 'Is that why you're paying me extra?'

Luke's eyes burned into hers, terrifying her by their ferocity as his grip on her hand tightened cruelly, reminding her forcefully of his strength, but she was beyond physical fear now.

'Because if that's the case it's not enough!' she cried sharply, wanting to hurt him as he had hurt her.

It seemed she had succeeded. Luke looked as if he had been struck, then he swung away from her so violently that the force of his movement sent her crashing into the wall as he stared out of the window, his hands thrust deep into his pockets, every muscle taut with tension.

'Dear God,' he said at last, his voice low and uneven. 'You seem determined to drive me mad! Jill——' As he turned back again he saw that she was carefully rubbing her arm where she had bruised it against the wall. Immediately his expression changed, his eyes darkening as all colour fled from his face. 'Did I hurt you?' he asked raggedly. 'I didn't mean to——'

The concern on his face almost disarmed her completely. 'Don't touch me!' she cried as he took a step towards her, but her voice did not have the force she wanted.

Luke held his hands up before him in a strangely defensive gesture. 'I won't,' he assured her hastily. 'I just wanted to apologise—— I never meant to hurt you.' His voice had changed on the last words, she realised dimly. He sounded almost as if he was talking about something other than her fall. She bent her head to hide her face. This was worse than ever! If he was going to start being kind to her she didn't think she could bear it.

'I'm quite all right,' she said stiffly. 'It's just a bruise, nothing more, nothing to worry about.' Nothing at all, she added miserably to herself, a tiny ache when compared to the raw, bleeding wound where her heart should be. 'But I think you'd better go now.'

'Of course.' The alacrity with which Luke agreed was inexpressibly hurtful. 'Just as long as you're sure about the job.'

'Quite sure.' She kept her head down, her face would give away too much if she looked at him. If he would just go she might hold herself together until she was alone.

'It was Paul's idea originally,' he astounded her by saying. 'He thought we could use a librarian.'

'What?' Jill's head came up swiftly, her aquamarine eyes widening in shock. 'I thought you wanted me to look after Danny!' she said sharply.

Suddenly it was as if the mask covering Luke's face had slipped and the raw emotion she saw in his eyes made her catch her breath.

'Just what sort of a job are you offering me?' she asked unsteadily. The silence while she waited for his answer seemed to last an eternity.

'*Anything*,' Luke said at last, his voice low and hoarse. 'Goddammit, Jill, anything at all, if you'll only come back!'

She found it very difficult to breathe. There seemed to be a tight knot in her throat as if all her feelings had caught there, choking her. 'For Danny's sake?' she managed, her voice croaking painfully.

'For Danny's sake if that's all you can manage—but I need you to be there so that I can see you, talk to you sometimes—nothing else, I promise you—I'll not force myself on you again.'

Jill couldn't believe what she was hearing. *I need you to*

*be there.* Could Luke really have said that?

'You didn't exactly force yourself on me,' she said softly, meeting his eyes at last. 'I was more than willing, and——' She broke off, unable to go on, unnerved by what she saw in his eyes, afraid to interpret it in case she was terribly wrong. Luke stood only feet away from her, but that distance seemed to stretch away into infinity. She wanted desperately to reach him but wasn't at all sure how to.

'Your money isn't what I want, Luke,' she said slowly and clearly, and his despondent sigh tore at her heart.

'I know.' His voice was so low she had to strain to hear it. 'I'm afraid I haven't quite cured myself of the habit of giving things instead of myself.'

For a moment his face blurred before her eyes as the full force of what he had said struck home, making her head reel.

'What are you *really* trying to say?' she questioned gently, and saw his head go back, a sudden flare of emotion lightening the darkness of his eyes.

'That I love you,' he said huskily.

'Oh, Luke!' Jill sighed her happiness. 'I love you too. But why did it take you so long to say it? It's such a simple thing.'

'Simple?' His smile was slow and rueful. 'Yes, to you I suppose it is—but my life isn't like that. Tony Atkins is just one of many, always at my heels, looking for a story, any story. That sort of publicity destroyed Marianne, and I didn't want another woman hurt in the same way—especially not someone like you. I thought I had it all worked out; if there was no woman in my life there'd be nothing for the press to write about—I was determined no other woman would have to endure all that again, so when I realised how much I was attracted to you, that I was coming back to Stoneroyd simply to see you I tried my damnedest to fight it.'

He glanced at her face and for a second there was a

flash of the old Luke in his eyes.

'And you were no bloody help, pestering me the way you did! It seemed that wherever I turned you were there, forcing me to think about you.' He sighed deeply and pushed his hand roughly through his hair. 'When you'd gone and I realised how wrong I'd been about Atkins I thought that at least you were safe from the press and in the end things would settle down again—go back to how they'd been before—but they didn't, not for me anyway. I'd fought it so hard from the moment I met you, but it had got the better of me. I can't fight it any more, I have to ask. I can't go back to Stoneroyd without you. Damn it, Jill, I'm asking for my own sake, not Danny's or anyone else's! Will you come and stay at Stoneroyd for ever—as my wife?'

No words were necessary; Jill's glowing face told him all he needed to know.

'I can think of nothing I'd like better in all the world,' she assured him in a voice that shook with happiness.

'Jill,' Luke's soft voice was equally uneven, and from the same cause, as he held out his arms to her, 'come here, because if I don't kiss you soon I *will* go mad!'

She went into his arms in a haze of contentment and, secure at last in Luke's love, his kiss was everything she had ever dreamed it would be. As he held her close to him she was oblivious to anything but him, the strength of his arms around her, the lean, hard body pressed so tightly against her. She didn't even notice when the door opened and her mother appeared in the doorway, a tray of coffee in her hands.

Seeing her daughter in the arms of the formidable gentleman who had appeared so unexpectedly on the doorstep, Mrs Carpenter hesitated, then silently withdrew. No doubt Jill would explain everything later. Neither Jill nor Luke saw her go.

A long time later Luke finally lifted his head and with Jill still cradled against him sighed his contentment.

'You needn't worry that I'll keep disappearing to London once we're married,' he told her gently. 'Those days are behind me now. I have the workroom all set up and Paul can manage the business side of things while I concentrate on my music and my family.' His eyes gleamed suddenly with wicked humour. 'Do you think you can handle a husband who's at home twenty-four hours a day, every day?'

Her answering smile delighted him with its innocent sensuality. 'I can handle it—it's just that I wonder how much work you'll actually get done!'

Her teasing was rewarded with a second, even more passionate kiss that turned her bones to water with the love and longing it revealed and its promise of so many delights to come. At long last Luke glanced reluctantly at his watch.

'We're going to have to go. I promised Danny and Lyne I'd be back at twelve—with you.'

'Were you so sure I'd say yes?' she asked, a mischievous smile curving her lips.

'No.' For a second his face lost its new-found happiness. 'But I was determined to bring you back to Stoneroyd, no matter what I had to do to get you there. I think I'd have used force if necessary.' Once more a grin lightened the sombre cast of his features. 'I wouldn't have dared face Danny if I'd had to go back without you!'

Jill's heart soared at the thought that she had come to mean so much to the little boy who had stolen her love from the first moment she had met him.

'Then we'd better go and put him out of his misery— he'll tear the house apart if we keep him waiting any longer.'

In the doorway Luke paused unexpectedly, drawing her back against him protectively as he regarded her seriously.

'There's one thing, little love. When our friend Atkins

gets to hear of this he's going to have a field day. Do you think you can cope?'

Jill's smile was confident and serene. 'I can cope with anything now,' she said. 'We'll cope with it together. And don't worry,' she added, wanting to remove the doubt that still clouded Luke's eyes. 'Remember, I now know just how underhand reporters can be. I'm not likely to believe any stories they might cook up in the future.'

'Well,' Luke's tone was wry, 'they've printed plenty of reports of my supposed romances that were totally false. It'll make a change for them to report the truth for once.' His hand moved up to touch her face very gently. 'It *is* true, isn't it?'

Jill turned her head until her lips rested against his hand and she pressed a kiss into his palm.

'Oh yes, my love,' she murmured. 'It's quite, quite true.

Every shadow fled from Luke's face as he slid an arm about her waist.

'Then nothing can touch us,' he declared smilingly. 'It'll all be just a nine days' wonder—and then we've all the rest of our lives ahead of us.'

'All the rest of our lives,' Jill echoed softly. The words had the most wonderful sound. She linked her hand with Luke's and together they walked away from the past and into that future.

# Harlequin Presents

## Coming Next Month

Available in March wherever paperback books are sold, or through
Harlequin Reader Service:

In the U.S.
901 Fuhrmann Blvd.
P.O. Box 1397
Buffalo, N.Y.  14240-1397

In Canada
P.O. Box 603
Fort Erie, Ontario
L2A 5X3

# Take 4 books
# & a surprise gift
# FREE

## SPECIAL LIMITED-TIME OFFER

Mail to    **Harlequin Reader Service®**

In the U.S.            In Canada
901 Fuhrmann Blvd.     P.O. Box 609
P.O. Box 1394         Fort Erie, Ontario
Buffalo, N.Y. 14240-1394  L2A 5X3

**YES!**    Please send me 4 free Harlequin Romance® novels and my free surprise gift. Then send me 8 brand-new novels every month as they come off the presses. Bill me at the low price of $1.99 each\*—an 11% saving off the retail price. There are no shipping, handling or other hidden costs. There is no minimum number of books I must purchase. I can always return a shipment and cancel at any time. Even if I never buy another book from Harlequin, the 4 free novels and the surprise gift are mine to keep forever.                           118 BPR BP7F

\*Plus 89¢ postage and handling per shipment in Canada.

| | |
|---|---|
| Name | (PLEASE PRINT) |
| Address | Apt. No. |
| City | State/Prov. | Zip/Postal Code |

This offer is limited to one order per household and not valid to present subscribers. Price is subject to change.     DOR-SUB-1D

A breathtaking roller coaster of adventure,
passion and danger in the dazzling
Roaring Twenties!

# SCANDALOUS SPIRITS

## ERIN YORKE

Running from unspeakable danger, she found shelter—and desire—
in the arms of a reckless stranger.

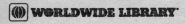